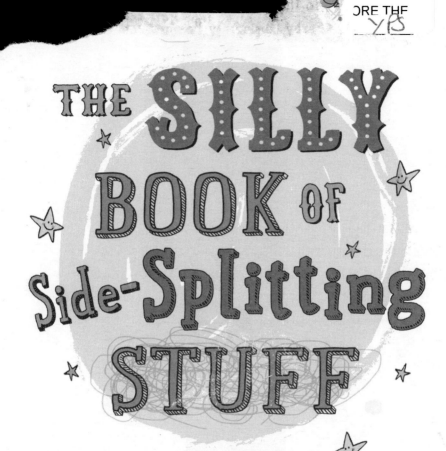

THE SILLY BOOK OF Side-Splitting STUFF

Illustrated by
Scott Garrett

BLOOMSBURY
LONDON OXFORD NEW YORK NEW DELHI SYDNE

To th
Amotherby Communit, Primary Schoo

Published 2014 by Bloomsbury Publishing Plc,
50 Bedford Square, London, WC1B 3DP
www.bloomsbury.com

Bloomsbury is a registered trademark of Bloomsbury Publishing Plc

ISBN 978-1-4088-5079-4

Copyright © 2014 Bloomsbury Publishing Plc
Text © 2014 Andy Seed
Illustrations © 2014 Scott Garrett
Additional illustrations © Shutterstock

A CIP record for this book is available from the British Library.

Printed and bound in Great Britain by CPI Group (UK) Ltd, Croydon CR0 4YY

7 9 10 8 6

MIX
Paper from
responsible sources
FSC® C020471
FSC
www.fsc.org

IMPORTANT:

The author and publisher recommend enabling
SafeSearch when using the Internet in conjuction
with this book. We can accept no responsibility
for information published on the Internet.

★ ★ ★ CONTENTS ★ ★ ★

★ ★ ★ ★ ★ ★ ★ ★ ★

INTRODUCTION

Adults are always telling children not to be silly. But the truth is that adults are often silly themselves, very silly! This book proves the matter. It's a collection of information and lists about silly people, inventions, food, names, sport and much, much more. If you read it, you'll find out just how silly grown ups sometimes are.

But it's not just about people: there are loads of funny facts about silly animals, silly words and silly places. Plus there are jokes, poems and things to do – all of them wonderfully silly!

SILLY ANIMALS

Potty pets

If you have ever had a pet you'll know that they have good days and bad days, just like their owners...

Cat burglar

A family from Bristol were confused when they kept finding strange items in their house: **dishcloths**, **T-shirts**, **boxer shorts** and a **sports bra**. It turned out that they had been stolen from neighbours' homes by their tabby cat, Norris. He also turned up with half a pizza, a tube of gravy paste and a German sausage. Bad kitty.

Mountie Python

Police were called to a hotel in Canada in 2013 to say that a couple staying there had gone, leaving their pets behind and that the staff couldn't deal with them. When the police arrived they discovered that the room contained forty snakes, all dangerous pythons.

Large fries and a shovel, please

A horse rider near Manchester was so cross that a McDonald's drive-through wouldn't serve her that she took her pony into the restaurant where it did a large poo on the floor. She was fined.

Big Boing

Nick Boing loved watching TV, going for car rides and walking to the shops (despite being a rather hefty 140kg in weight). His favourite food was carrots and he lived in a bungalow in Wales. Oh, and he was a pet sheep.

Call the vet

A large Doberman dog from South Africa called Nero was keen for his owner to take him on lots of walks. When he noticed that she was on her mobile a lot, Nero decided to do something about it. He ate the phone.

Batty birds

These birds are not silly – they just sound like they have silly names.
The countries in brackets are good places to see them.

Noisy leatherhead
(Australia)

Bare-faced go-away bird
(Tanzania)

Spotted thick knee
(Ethiopia)

Blue-footed booby
(Peru)

Laughing jackass
(New Zealand)

Golden-rumped tinkerbird
(Congo)

Gang gang cockatoo
(Australia)

Yellow-bellied sapsucke
(Canada)

Purple grackle
(USA)

Zany zoo tales

Are you lion?

In China, a mother and son visiting Louhe Zoo were very surprised to hear a lion bark. The creature in the cage, labelled as an 'African lion', turned out to be a shaggy Tibetan mastiff dog.

Monkey see, monkey go

In 1935 a zoo attendant at an animal park in New York used a plank to cross a wall and stinky moat over to the large monkey colony to do some cleaning. While his back was turned, about 170 monkeys escaped using the plank and headed into the city, raiding fruit wherever they went. Whoops.

Bear cheek

Zookeepers at Knoxville were very surprised when they saw a large black bear climbing the zoo's high perimeter fence. This was a wild bear and for some reason the silly animal was breaking into the zoo...

Slippery penguin

A small penguin once escaped from Tokyo Sea Life Park by somehow climbing a four-metre wall and some barbed wire. Normally, escaped animals are recaptured the same day but this cheeky bird enjoyed freedom for over two months, snacking on fish in Tokyo Bay.

Amusing animals

Well, whoever named these poor beasties was having an attack of the sillies:

Pudu (small deer)

Flat-headed myotis (bat)

Aye-aye (lemur)

Obese lily weevil (beetle)

Bongo (antelope)

Aha ha (wasp)

Tiny tuco-tuco (rodent)

Crappie (fish)

Latin loopiness

Many animals have two names: a common name and a scientific name (sometimes known as a Latin name). Some of the scientific names sound pleasingly nutty, as you'll see from this selection:

Scientific name	Common name
Bufo bufo	Toad
Elephas maximus	Asian elephant
Llama glama	Llama
Bombus confusus	A type of bumblebee
Pica pica	Magpie
Lynx lynx	Lynx
Ursus arctos horribilis	Grizzly bear
Gorilla gorilla gorilla	Western lowland gorilla
Parastratiosphecomyia sphecomyioides	Soldier fly

Crazy creatures

The things these animals do are probably very sensible to them but to most people they are right up there on the silly scale:

Frogs	Drink through their skin.
Horned lizards	Able to shoot blood from their eyes.
Clams	Can change from male to female.
Naked mole rats	Eat their own poo.
Starfish	If they get too hot they can lose an arm.
Crocodiles	Swallow stones.
Lobsters	When kept in a tank with no food they will eat themselves.
Scorpions	Some types glow in the dark when there's a full moon.
Pythons	Occasionally eat animals so large that their skin bursts.
Raft spider	Chases prey across water.

Nonsensical names

Some animals' names are silly because they are confusing. Have a look at these and you'll see what I mean:

Starfish	It's not a fish.
Horny toad	It's a lizard, not a toad.
Electric eel	It's not an eel but a knifefish.
Mountain goat	Although it does live on mountains it's not a goat.
Guinea pig	They're not from Guinea and they're not pigs.
Flying lemur	It's not a lemur and it can't fly (OK, it can glide a bit).
Black rhino	It's not black.
White rhino	It's not white.

Mythological monsters

The Ancient Greeks loved a good beastie and here are some of the sillier ones from their fabulous tales of heroes, gods and magic fruit:

Centaur — Had a man's head and body with a horse's legs and bum. (Had a hard time finding jeans to fit.)

Gorgon — Foul tempered lady-beast with hair made of snakes. (Try getting shampoo for *that*.)

Ladon — A snaky dragon whose job it was to guard golden apples. (Apart from the murderous tendencies, he's lovely.)

Hydra — Reptilian brute of multiple bonces and venomous breath. (Rarely invited to weddings.)

Cerberus — Three-headed hound that watched over the gates of hell. (You'll need a *lot* of doggie treats.)

Manticore — Man's head, lion's body and a tail that could shoot spikes. (The kind of boyfriend that mums adore.)

Cyclops — One-eyed man-munching giants who tend sheep. (Avoid for babysitting.)

Celeb cats

Some people are a bit silly when it comes to cats...

Anfield Cat

Tabby that walked onto the pitch during a Liverpool FC match. Has almost 60,000 followers on Twitter.

Blackie

The 'world's richest cat', left £9m by his owner when he died.

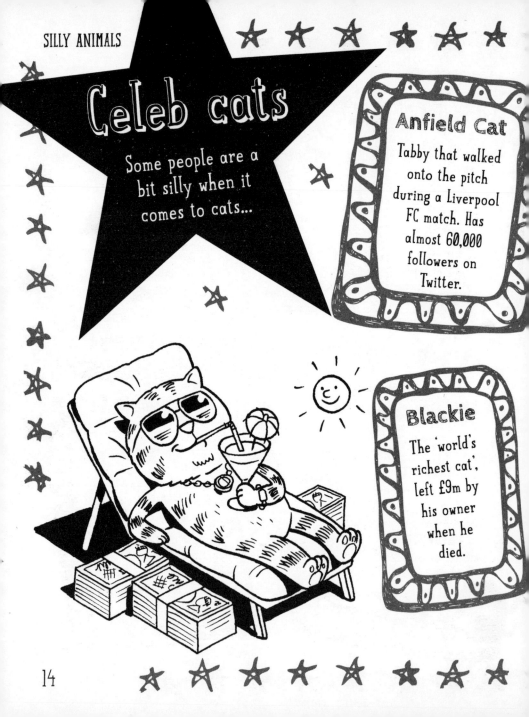

Casper

A cat who travelled 11 miles each day on a bus in Plymouth all by himself. He wasn't charged.

Stubbs

A tail-less cat elected mayor of Talkeelna, a town in Alaska, USA.

Mike

A cat who guarded the gates of the British Museum from 1909–1929 and has his own tombstone in London.

Grumpy Cat

An Internet and TV star, famous for looking cross. There is a Grumpy Cat Facebook page with over seven million likes, and an official book.

Lil Bub

A dwarf cat described as 'the world's cutest'. She has no teeth, extra toes and a range of merchandise.

Blend-a-beast

You can have fun mixing together animals to make up new silly ones. After all, it's been done before: a liger (lion + tiger) and Batman (bat + human). Here's a few to get you started:

Gibbon + piglet = **giblet**

House martin + donkey = **housekey**

Chicken + magpie = **chicken pie**

Horse + rabbit = **hobbit**

Stingray + skunk = **stink**

Pug + anteater = **panteater**

Wombat + cricket = **cricket bat**

Dingo + dugong = **dingdong**

Marten + wolverine = **margarine**

Earwig + waxwing = **earwax**

Hare + cuttlefish = **harecut**

Marmot + termite = **marmite**

Draw your own blend-a-beast here:

SILLY PLACES
Eccentric homes

It's well worth doing an Internet image search to find pictures of these excellent houses from around the world.

The Upside-Down House

This small wooden house in Szymbark, Poland was built, er, upside down. Its designer wanted to say something about the crazy backwardness of the world that we live in. With the roof at the bottom and hanging furniture stuck above everyone's head, it's certainly crazy.

Walking house

This is the perfect home if you don't like your neighbours – it's a metal box with windows, built on six hydraulic legs. Made by Danish students, the house has a computer which allows it to move around and avoid floods.

The Toilet House

This house in South Korea is round, white and shaped like a loo, complete with a hollow centre. It was built in 2007 to celebrate the first meeting of the World Toilet Association.

The Dunmore Pineapple

A large stone summer house built over 200 years ago by the wealthy Earl of Dunmore in Scotland which looks like a giant pineapple. The story goes that the Earl was so amazed by pineapples he found growing in America that he ordered a building shaped like one.

The Headington Shark

2, New High Street, Headington, Oxford is an ordinary-looking brick terraced house, except that it has a seven-metre shark sticking out of its roof. The plastic beast is a sculpture.

The Winchester Mystery House

This bonkers mansion in California took 36 years to build because the owner kept adding bits on without any plans. It has 160 rooms, 467 doorways and staircases which lead nowhere. It has also survived two earthquakes and is supposed to be haunted.

Silly UK villages

OK, they're not really silly, but their names sure are to some people!

Barton in the Beans	Leicestershire
Boghead	Scotland
Cow Ark	Lancashire
Killiecrankie	Scotland
Nasty	Hertfordshire
Pant	Shropshire
Six-Mile Bottom	Suffolk
Turner's Puddle	Dorset
World's End	Berkshire

Silly street names

These are all in Britain:

Batman Close

Cracknuts Lane

Elvis Road

Land of Green Ginger

Man in the Moon Passage

Whip-Ma-Whop-Ma-Gate

Even more silly UK places

Bare	A part of Morecambe, Lancashire
Blubberhouses	A moor in North Yorkshire
Booby Dingle	A valley in Herefordshire
Funzie	A bay in Shetland, Scotland
Hen Poo	A lake near Berwick-upon-Tweed
Horrid Hill	A hill in Kent
Loose Bottom	A valley in Sussex
Splott	A district of Cardiff

You built it where?

These are all examples of buildings which are in silly places.

Stott Hall Farm

This is an old farmhouse in the hills of West Yorkshire in the UK. Nothing unusual about that, except that it's in the central reservation of the M62 motorway.

House in the highway

Stott Hall Farm isn't actually in the road but poor Luo Baogen's house in China was. The local government decided to build a highway where his house was but he refused to sell it so they built the road anyway, leaving the house right in the middle!

Fort Roughs

This is a small platform in the North Sea, built in World War II. In 1967 it was seized by a man called Paddy Bates who declared it as an independent state called Sealand. There have been several crazy battles involving people trying to grab the fort.

Manaus Opera House

This is a large, old, ornate opera house. It has 198 chandeliers and is in the middle of the Amazon rainforest.

Fallingwater

This is a famous modern house in America. And it's built on top of a waterfall. 'Nuff said.

Daniel's column

Daniel the Stylite was a holy man living in Turkey from 409 BC. He made a stone column his home and stood on it for 33 years. Don't ask me why.

Wacky hotels

Fancy a memorable holiday this year?

Wallett's Court Tipis, UK

Native American tipis with beds, fire pits and reindeer skins.

Jules Undersea Lodge, USA

An underwater hotel in a lagoon – you need to dive to get in.

Hotel Parchi de Garda, Italy

Has four animatronic rooms including one with a wall which has eyes and a mouth that talks.

Sala Silvermine, Sweden

A hotel built 155m underground which includes the world's deepest bedroom.

Free Spirit Spheres, Canada

Giant balls hanging from trees in a Canadian forest, with beds but not a lot else.

Jumbo Stay, Sweden

A hotel in a Boeing 747 Jumbo Jet — you can even sleep in the cockpit!

Godiva Chocolate Suite, USA

A hotel room made from chocolate, yes even the chairs, bed and walls. Probably didn't last long...

The Ice Hotel, Sweden

All the rooms are made of ice but it has to be rebuilt each year after melting. Cool.

The Sandcastle Hotel, England

In 2008 a hotel was built on Weymouth beach from 1,000 tons of sand. It was cheap to stay in, but unfortunately there was no roof, no toilets and the whole thing soon washed away.

Fun fictional towns

These towns are from books, films and TV and none of them are real.
Just as well.

Gotham City
The haunt of Batman and numerous nasty villains.

Trumpton
Happening animated town of the 60s where Chippy Minton lives.

Puddleby-on-the-Marsh
Home of Dr Dolittle who can talk to the animals, no less.

Ffarquhar
Jolly town at the end of Thomas the Tank Engine's branch line.

New New York
From the zany American cartoon series *Futurama*.

Smurf Village
Where the comic little blue fellows live.

Ballykissangel
The rather lovely setting for an Irish telly drama series.

Pontypandy
Welsh town where Fireman Sam's fire station is.

Death
Unappealing city on the planet of Jubilar in *Star Wars*.

Bikini Bottom
The underwater home of dippy submariner Spongebob Squarepants.

Silly festivals

...around the world

La Tomatina

A giant tomato fight which happens every August in Buñol in Spain. About 150,000 squashed tomatoes are thrown at everyone and anything by 20,000 people. Yay!

Running of the bulls

Held each July in the Spanish city of Pamplona, this involves foolhardy folk running in front of six bulls that charge through the streets of the town along a set route. Each year 200–300 people are injured, including some gored by horns. Ouch.

Other silly festivals

World Gurning Championships (UK)
A face-pulling contest usually won by toothless old men.

Tunarama (Australia)
People toss a dead tuna fish as far as they can.

Boryeong Mud Festival (South Korea)
A truly monster mud fight.

Silly places to go

If you fancy a nice day out then avoid these locations: they are some of the most dangerous places in the world.

Annapurna

Annapurna in Asia is the tenth highest mountain in the world at 8,091 metres and probably the most dangerous. Only about 190 people have managed to climb it and over 60 have died trying.

Zambezi

This African river is 2,200 miles long and has killer rapids, big rocks, whirlpools, deep water and unexploded mines, not to mention the 108m high Victoria Falls, the world's largest waterfall. You'll also find hungry crocs, moody hippos and even bull sharks in the lower reaches. Yikes.

Antarctica

This wilderness of ice, snow and mountains is the planet's coldest place with temperatures reaching minus 60 degrees and winds which often blow at 100km/h. There are no hotels, shops or hospitals. There aren't even any trees to shelter under.

South China Sea

There have been 293 shipping accidents here in the last fifteen years, plus you might come across cyclones (tropical storms) and earthquakes which cause tsunamis (giant waves), as well as armed modern-day pirates.

Merapi

The name of this rumbling volcano in Indonesia means 'mountain of fire' and it has erupted regularly over the last 500 years, producing more flows of red-hot lava than any other. Just to make things worse there are also regular earthquakes in the area. Avoid.

Louisiana Swamps

In this part of the USA, you'll find large alligators, deadly cottonmouth snakes, snapping turtles, biting insects, sinking mud and dangerous plants like poison ivy. But apart from those it's fine.

Taklamakan Desert

Legend has it that the ancient name of this vast desert in China means 'you go in but don't come out'. It's certainly big, at 960km across, waterless, and baking hot in the day but freezing at night. The other main dangers are becoming lost due to the shifting sand dunes or being buried by blinding sandstorms which also hurl stones. And watch out for the scorpions!

Amazon rainforest

It's easy to get lost in the world's largest rainforest but you're more likely to get sick from insect bites or drinking dirty water. Then there are the blood-sucking leeches, the piranhas in the water, the jaguars, anacondas and venomous spiders. Oh, and the floods.

Bizarre American towns

★ ★ ★ ★ ★ ★ ★ ★ ★

It's not just people in the UK who have a habit of choosing unusual names for their towns. People in the USA have chosen some great names for the places they live:

Pie Town (New Mexico)
Handsome Eddy (New York)
Looneyville (West Virginia)
Hungry Horse (Montana)
Cranky Corner (Louisiana)
Ding Dong (Texas)
Kickapoo (Illinois)

Drab (Pennsylvania)
Boring (Oregon)
No Name (Colorado)
Zap (North Dakota)
Wimp (California)
Muck City (Alabama)
Stinking Bay (Arkansas)

Six startling facts about the Eiffel Tower

All true!

- The Eiffel Tower is over 1 metre tall.

- If you climbed the Eiffel Tower by the steps, starting at 9 a.m. and going at 48 steps a minute without stopping, you'd be very tired.

- The tower is not made from pastry.

- The Eiffel Tower took several people quite a long time to build.

- The Eiffel Tower has never been to Luton.

- There are no plans at present to coat the Eiffel Tower in breadcrumbs.

SILLY HISTORY
A few eccentrics

Eccentrics are people, often rich, who behave in silly ways but they don't regard themselves as being silly. Here are some eccentrics from history:

Jeremy Bentham (philosopher)

Bentham had himself mummified when he died. His clothed body is now kept in a cupboard at University College London, although his head is mostly made of wax as the real one went a bit manky.

Horace de Vere Cole (prankster)

This wealthy joker once threw a party and only invited people who had 'bottom' in their surname.

The 5th Duke of Portland (aristocrat)

A mega-shy person who never spoke to anyone, he built a pink underground mansion which had a library 76m long. If the duke went out he hid under an extra-large umbrella.

Cyrus Teed (scientist)

He promoted the Hollow Earth theory which claimed that people live on the inside of the planet rather than the outside and that the sun was a giant battery.

Howard Hughes (billionaire)

An aircraft designer who acted strangely as he became older, sitting in the nude and watching the same film 150 times. He once ordered 1,300 litres of banana nut ice cream.

Quack cures

A quack is a person who falsely claims to have medical knowledge. These tricksters operated widely in the 1800s selling useless or dangerous 'quack medicines' which contained cheap ingredients and were sold at a profit. Here are some examples:

Snake Oil
Claimed to cure:
Joint pains
Included ingredients:
Oil, beef fat and turpentine

Daffy's Elixir
Claimed to cure:
Wind
Included ingredients:
Lots of things, including crushed beetles and rhubarb

Crosby's Brain Food
Claimed to cure:
Nervous exhaustion
Included ingredients:
Wheat and ox brain

Wizard Oil
Claimed to cure:
Toothache and cancer
Included ingredients:
Mainly alcohol, plus spices like cloves

Revalenta Arabica
Claimed to cure:
Many sicknesses
Included ingredients:
Lentil flour

Microbe Killer
Claimed to cure:
All diseases'
Included ingredients:
Water, acid and wine

Dr Watson's Worm Syrup
Claimed to cure:
Worms
Included ingredients:
Unknown

Peculiar jobs

Silly work was once a lot easier to find – just look at this lot:

Knocker-up
Before alarm clocks some people would hire a man or woman to wake them up by banging on their window or door in the morning. A stick was usually used but some knockers-up used a pea shooter!

Gong farmer
This unfortunate person would work in the night emptying human excrement from the pits that people used before toilets were invented. In Tudor times some were paid sixpence a day for being up to their knees in stinky poo.

Rat catcher
In Victorian days one occupation involved catching live rats which were then often sold for illegal dog vs rat fights. The rats were caught by hand and often carried nasty diseases...

Whipping boy
Five hundred years ago each time a prince in England was naughty and deserved punishment another boy called the whipping boy would get whacked instead. This was because the future king was not allowed to be punished. Seems a tad unfair.

Body snatcher
In the past people learning to be doctors urgently needed dead bodies to practise on and so they paid illegal body snatchers to dig up freshly buried corpses from graveyards at night.

Silly rulers

Kings, emperors, sultans, chiefs, lords, Pharaohs, presidents, czars... you would think they'd choose sensible ones. Oh no...

Nero

Nero was a Roman Emperor who did lots of very silly things. He married his stepsister, killed his mother and set fire to Christians. He also won a chariot race at the Ancient Olympics even though he fell out of the chariot.

Attila the Hun

Attila was a ruler of a huge area of Asia and Europe in the 400s. His favourite pastime was invading and his fearsome Hun army conquered the lands of the Goths, Celts, Romans and many more. Attila killed his brother and then invaded Italy where he died mysteriously after he had a bad nose bleed.

Leopold II

Leopold was King of Belgium from 1865 to 1909. He sent a team of explorers to Africa to claim land for himself and he established his own personal country there, the Congo Free State. Leopold became very rich, forcing the natives to work and grabbing all the ivory and rubber he could. Lazy workers had a hand cut off.

Ivan the Terrible

Ivan the Terrible's grandfather was known as Ivan the Great but the younger Ivan was definitely not great, he was, er, terrible. He was ruler of Russia in the 1500s and got his way by creating a force of nasty secret police who dressed in black and went round biffing people. In a rage he also bopped his son on the head with a stick, which killed the poor boy. Terrible.

Justin II

This fellow was Eastern Roman Emperor about 1,500 years ago. He wasn't very successful as a ruler, and turned insane as he became older. One historian reports that he was pulled through his palace on a wheeled throne, biting servants as he passed. There was also a rumour that he ate two of them.

Silly British laws from bygone days

Over the last 1,000 years, Britain has had some very peculiar laws, as this little list demonstrates.

In 1307 any whale washed up on the shore belonged to the king.

A law of 1541 required every Englishman between the ages of 17 and 60 to keep a longbow and practise archery.

The Puritans, led by Oliver Cromwell in the 1600s, banned the celebration of Christmas.

It was against the law in Puritan times to go for a walk on a Sunday, unless to church.

In 1774 it was an offence to keep more than one lunatic without a licence for a madhouse.

It became illegal to carry a plank along a London pavement in 1839. This is still in force.

The Town Police Clauses Act of 1847 banned people from sliding on ice or snow.

The law above also outlawed shaking a carpet in the street.

The Salmon Act of 1986 states that it is illegal to 'handle salmon in suspicious circumstances'.

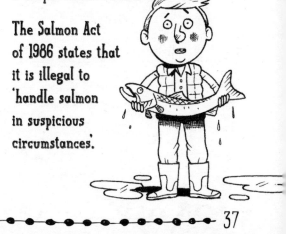

Daft annual traditions of the UK

Great Britain probably has more barmy customs than any other country. Here are some good ones:

The Haxey Hood
(began 1300s)

A bonkers giant rugby scrum where villagers try and push a leather hood into one of four pubs. It features people dressed as a Lord, a Fool and eleven Boggins, whatever they are.

The Burning of Bartle
(began possibly 1500s)

A scary clothed dummy is paraded through the streets of a Yorkshire village each August. A load of nonsense rhymes are chanted along the way then the poor dummy is set on fire.

Royal Shrovetide Football
(began 1200s or earlier)

A wild, giant game played by hundreds of people in the town of Ashbourne, with goals three miles apart on a riverbank. It lasts two days. The game is so rough that most of the town's shops are boarded up.

Padstow Obby Oss
(began 1700s possibly)

A May Day custom in Cornwall featuring two scary black panto-style 'hobby horses' who parade through the town trying to grab young girls. As always there's lots of singing involved.

Cooper's Hill Cheese Rolling (began 1800s)

People injure themselves chasing a large round cheese down a very steep hill. It is so dangerous that it was banned in 2010 but local people carried on doing it anyway.

The Straw Bear (began 1800s)

A man wears a costume made of straw and dances through the town of Whittlesey while locals give him money and food. The costume is then burnt.

Whuppity Scoorie (began 1800s)

Children of Lanark in Scotland run round the church whirling big balls of paper on the end of strings then they are thrown money by people of the town. It's all to welcome in spring, they reckon.

Other wacky British customs and traditions held each year include:

* Hallaton Bottle Kicking
* The World Pooh Sticks Championship
* Gravy Wrestling
* The Nettle-eating Contest
* Fireball-whirling
* The Nutters Dance, Bacup
* Custard Pie Throwing Championships
* Worm Charming
* Shin-kicking

The Great Stink

1858 was not a good year to be in London. Why? Read on and you'll find out about a silly situation that became a smelly and dangerous one.

Victorian London was a very busy city with hundreds of thousands of people all living and working close together. Where there's lots of people, there's lots of poo, and in 1858 this was a big problem.

The flushing toilet had just become popular and the easiest place for people to flush away their stinky waste was into the River Thames. As well as sewage the river was also where people dumped dead animals, horse manure and nasty chemicals from factories.

Things became really bad in the year 1858 when there was a heatwave. The hot sun dried up the Thames and the river could no longer wash away all the poo. Ponking piles were left on the riverbanks, slowly cooking in the summer warmth, and the overpowering stench enveloped the whole city. It was called 'The Great Stink'.

London smelt like a giant toilet and Members of Parliament meeting in the newly built House of Commons next to the river found that the pong was so strong that they couldn't work. In between wafts they arranged for new sewers to be built.

Eventually rains came and washed away the mounds of metropolitan muck but no one would ever forget what was possibly the worst whiff in history.

Potty punishments

You really, really didn't want to be a criminal in the past. The kind of sentences that were dealt out were just a teeny bit harsh, as you'll see from this list.

In Ancient Egypt slaves who escaped sometimes had their nose cut off.

In medieval times, liars and thieves were often put in a pillory – a wooden or metal device which locked the person's head and hands in place in a standing up position. The pillory was placed in public so that the offender could be humiliated and pelted with mouldy veg.

The Aztecs of the 1500s in Mexico were not to be messed with. A person found to be drunk would end up with a shaved head and his or her house would be destroyed.

The 'Bloody Code' of the 1770s allowed the death penalty for stealing goods worth more than 12 pence.

During the 18th and 19th centuries, approximately 162,000 convicts were transported to Australia by ship for crimes such as cutting down an apple tree.

1752:
the silliest year

Here are some curious facts about the year 1752:

In Britain it should have been 366 days long (it was a leap year) but it was only 355 days.

Eleven days were removed from the year in order to make Britain's calendar match that in other European countries.

There was no September 3rd, 4th, 5th, 6th, 7th, 8th, 9th, 10th, 11th, 12th or 13th that year, so if it was your birthday then, tough!

People went to sleep on the evening of September 2nd and woke up next morning on September 14th – this confused a lot of people, not surprisingly, especially as there was no radio, TV or Internet to explain what was going on, and many couldn't read the newspapers.

Up to this year, New Year's Day in Britain was 1st April. In 1752 it switched to 1st January.

Many people disliked the new New Year and refused to change, so the king (George II) declared that those who held New Year on April 1st would be fools.

HAPPY *NEW* YEAR

SILLY FOOD

Full of nuts
Strange chocolate bars

There are hundreds of chocolate bars made all over the world and some of them have very silly names. But remember, Twix might be a totally hilarious name in Japan or Peru... Anyway, here are some real choccy bars from the around the planet:

Action Max Turkey

Hum Hum Syria

Milk Duds Canada

Oh Henry! USA

Turbo India

Plopp Sweden

Perky Nana New Zealand

Ludicrous banquets

Many rulers from the past loved their food and took great pleasure from showing off by ordering gigantic feasts for hundreds of guests. Here are four of the most gigantic:

Nero's bash

This potty Roman emperor regularly threw huge rude parties and gorged himself on such things as dormice, boiled calf and pigs' udders washed down with unlimited drink.

The Field of the Cloth of Gold

England and France were at war for much of history but in the year 1520 Henry VIII (the six-wife king) met up with Francis I to make friends and try and out-do each other with how rich and powerful they were. The result was mountains of food and a wine fountain.

The Medici Wedding

When a later king of France married the daughter of Italy's richest family in 1600, the wedding guests enjoyed one of the largest knees-ups of all time, including a meal with over fifty courses.

The Regent's banquet

The Prince Regent of England ordered an outrageous feast in 1817 to celebrate the visit of the Grand Duke of Russia to his snazzy palace in Brighton. In total there were 120 dishes including a metre-high marzipan temple for afters.

Gross groceries:
Disgusting foods from around the world?

Would you eat these?

Rat Stew (China)
Poo coffee (Philippines)
Sheep's Head (Norway)
Maggot Cheese (Sardinia)
Raw Blood Soup (Vietnam)
Tuna Eyeball (Japan)
Bird Spit (China)
Monkey Brains (Indonesia)

Yucky survival foods*

If you're stuck alone on a desert island (it's bound to happen one day) or lost in the woods with no pies or caramel cake then what can you eat? Well, some types of these is the answer:

Worms
Grasshoppers
Ants
Nettles
Inner pine tree bark

Frogs
Scorpions
Cockroaches
Seaweed

*Don't actually try these!

How much gravy can they hold?

If you're like the author of this book, you've probably spent a long time wondering just how much gravy can be poured into things. Well, now you know.

Sock	0.8 bowls
The FA Cup	12 bowls
Mini Cooper Convertible (boot)	330 bowls
A bath	360 bowls
Fridge-freezer	784 bowls
Double bedroom	80,000 bowls
Olympic-sized swimming pool	2 million bowls
Boeing Everett Factory	26.6 billion bowls
Loch Ness	14,800,000,000,000 bowls, or thereabouts

Don't eat that, Nigel!

Most people eat only food but some people have been known to supplement their diet with other things:

Tarrare

Tarrare was a French soldier of the 1700s who was always hungry. He could swallow apples whole, stones and even live animals such as snakes and lizards. He was taken to hospital to try and cure his habits but they found him tucking into a dead body in the mortuary.

Mr Mangetout

Michel Lolito from France was an entertainer who consumed metal as part of his act. Altogether he ate 18 bikes, seven TVs, two beds and a small aircraft. He died in 2007.

Charles Domery

This gent was a Polish soldier of the 19th century who could eat almost anything. Unhappy with his large rations he would sometimes chomp 2kg of grass a day and once finished a meal cooked for 15 people. He was put in jail where he ate 20 rats, the prison cat and several candles.

'You ate what?'

Doctors across the world have X-rayed patients who were complaining of tummy aches only to find they have swallowed something silly. The following items have been found in people's stomachs: rocks, toys, batteries, a fork, car keys and glass.

Suspicious supermarket products

☛ Reduced fat socks

☛ Non-stick grapes

☛ Organic batteries

☛ Traditional petrol

☛ Crinkle-cut milk

☛ Free-range toilet paper

SILLY PEOPLE

Whoops!

Here is a little collection of gaffes and blunders by various people from around the planet.

Inn trouble

In 2012 it was reported that a British family with three children went to have Sunday lunch in a pub. They enjoyed the meal, went home by car and then noticed that they'd only returned with two children. They'd left their eight-year-old daughter Nancy at the pub. Oh, and the father was British Prime Minister David Cameron.

Act stupid

Marilyn Monroe was a huge film star in the 1950s but it was said she had trouble remembering her lines. For one film she was supposed to find a bottle in a drawer. Apparently, she got the line wrong over 40 times so the director wrote the words on a piece of paper and put it in the drawer. Marilyn tried again and walked across the room to open the drawer. Unfortunately she went to the wrong drawer.

Potty prof

Paul Erdös was a very clever Professor of Mathematics, but apparently once at a meeting and talking to a man...

'Where are you from?' said Paul.

'Vancouver,' said the man.

'Oh, then you must know my good friend Elliot Mendelson,' said Paul. The man replied, 'I am your good friend Elliot Mendelson.'

Personal parcel

Charles McKinley wanted to visit his father in Dallas but couldn't afford the plane ticket from his home in New York, over 1,300 miles away. So, instead, he hid in a crate and had himself mailed to save money. He was discovered by the delivery driver in Dallas and then arrested by the police.

Dan the Spud

Dan Quayle was Vice President of the USA in 1992 when he visited a school that was holding a Spelling Bee competition. According to reports a twelve-year-old boy called William correctly wrote the word 'potato' but Mr Quayle told him it was wrong and should be written 'potatoe'.

Silly careers?

Choosing a job is always tricky. You could become a chef or a doctor but why not opt for something more interesting? These jobs are all real:

Chicken sexer	This person looks closely at little fluffy chicks to see if they are male or female.
Scatologist	A scientist who studies poo. Yes, it's examined for clues about diet, health, etc.
Banana gasser	Someone who sprays green bananas with gas to make them ripe for the shops.
Pet food taster	A person who, well, eats dog and cat food to see what it tastes like. Yum....
Snake milker	Someone brave who collects the poisonous venom from deadly snakes.
Vomit cleaner	A poor soul who works at theme park rides clearing up you-know-what.
Cheese sprayer	This job involves spraying melted cheese onto popcorn in a factory.
Sniffologist	Somebody who tests deodorants by smelling people's armpits all day. Nice.
Professional zombie	A person who pretends to be undead in a dungeon tourist attraction.
Glass eye maker	An expert who makes fake eyes for people who have lost a real one.

Famous pranks

Practical jokes are fun and very silly. There are small ones and there are BIG ones, like these (all true and mostly performed on April fool's day):

In 1860 people in London were invited to view the annual ceremony of Washing the White Lions at the Tower of London. By noon a large crowd had gathered at the tower. They soon discovered that there were no lions at the tower, let alone white lions.

Burger King put out a full-page newspaper advert in 1998 announcing a new item on their menu: the Left-Handed Whopper, specially designed for left-handed Americans. Thousands of customers asked for the new burger, while many others wanted a 'right-handed' one.

In 1957 the serious BBC TV programme Panorama featured the 'spaghetti harvest' in Switzerland. It showed a family pulling pasta off trees and putting it in baskets. The hoax fooled thousands of viewers, some of whom rang in to ask where they could buy a spaghetti tree.

One April morning in 1974, people in Sitka, Alaska were horrified to see thick smoke rising from the top of the nearby volcano, Mount Edgecumbe, thinking it might be about to erupt. It turned out that the smoke was from a pile of car tyres which had been set on fire by local joker Porky Bickar.

One night in 1998 students in California, USA, replaced 76 outdoor chairs at a university café with 76 toilets which had been taken out of a nearby building for disposal.

A newspaper from Denmark reported in 1965 that the Danish parliament had changed the law and now required that all dogs must be painted white. This was a road safety measure, it said, and would ensure that dogs could be seen more easily at night.

During the year 2000, motorists travelling along the M3 in Hampshire were surprised to see a new zebra crossing on the very busy motorway. An unknown prankster had painted it during the night.

A list of annoying people

These are all people to avoid, but do you know what they all mean?

Party pooper
Smart alec
Oaf
Embezzler
Ruffian
Bossy boots
Kvetch
Charlatan
Hustler
Gasbag
Snoot
Blabbermouth
Lout
Snob
Philistine
Prophet of doom
Loose cannon
Scrounger

Rubbernecker
Control freak
Sourpuss
Pedant
Despot
Phony
Hanger on
Backstabber
Grouch
Stooge
Braggart
Spoilsport
Jobsworth
Fuddy-duddy
Oik
Nitpicker
Fop
N'er-do-well

Spiv
Shyster
Henchman
Flash harry
Gatecrasher
Quack
Buffoon
Poser
Prude
Scaremonger
Hoodlum
Killjoy
Fraud
Stickler
Stick-in-the-mud
Eavesdropper
Wastrel
Fusspot

Fun fictional characters

Here is a wondrous mix of characters from comics, TV, books, cartoons and myths. They are all interesting, amusing, entertaining and occasionally silly.

The BFG
Roald Dahl's 24-foot tall giant has humungous ears, eats snozzcumbers and trumps a lot.

Goldfinger
A greedy Bond villain obsessed with gold who has a hat-throwing henchman called Oddjob.

The Tiger who Came to Tea
A tiger mysteriously turns up at a little girl's house, eats all the food, drinks everything then vanishes. Curious.

Wonder Woman
A superhero warrior princess who has two bulletproof bracelets and a razor-sharp tiara.

Bertie Wooster
An empty-headed posh English gent, Bertie is constantly rescued from scrapes by his shrewd butler, Jeeves.

Tom
Manic, foolish and death-defying animated cat whose life is spent pursuing crafty mouse Jerry.

Miss Trunchbull
Fearsome, muscular, pigtail-hating headteacher from Roald Dahl's story, *Matilda*.

Bottom
A Shakespeare comedy character who gets his head turned into a donkey's by a cheeky fairy.

Gollum
A scary bug-eyed creature who finds a powerful ring and hunts the hobbit who takes it.

Nigel Molesworth
Boy-hero and anti-speller of St Custard's who features in the book *Down With Skool*.

Minnie the Minx
Mischievous girl from legendary comic *The Beano*, who wears a red and black striped jumper.

Riddler
Villainous enemy of Batman, the mega-smart Riddler loves puzzles, tricks and word games.

Mary Poppins
Flying nanny of book and film who uses magic to give her family's kids a tea party on the ceiling.

Wicked Witch of the West
A bad sorceress from the land of Oz who has a pack of winged monkeys among other nasties.

Noddy Boffin
One of Charles Dickens' characters, a kindly servant who inherits a fortune but turns greedy.

Desperate Dan
Ludicrously strong Wild West buffoon from *The Dandy* comic, who loves munching cow pie.

An unusual act...

'Le Petomane' was the stage name of a man who had one of the silliest stage acts in the history of show business.

Real name: Joseph Pujol
Nationality: French
Born: 1857
Died: 1945
Occupation: professional farter
Performed in: theatres, mainly in Paris

Famous trump-based impressions: animals, various people, tearing cloth, a cannon, thunder
Other bottom talents: 'playing' songs, extinguishing a candle
Once performed for: the King of Belgium
Translation of Le Petomane: 'The Fartiste'

SILLY INVENTIONS

Wacky patents

The world is full of madcap inventors generating ideas for things that not everybody wants. All of these people have one thing in common: they hate the thought of others stealing their inventions. This is why we have patents: a patent protects an idea so that people can't legally copy it. All of the following ideas have been officially registered in this way:

Gerbil shirt

A curious vest covered in loops of wide plastic tubing so that a gerbil can crawl all over you when you visit Aunt Periwinkle.

Three-legged pantyhose

Nylon tights often do 'ladder' so why not wear a pair with an extra leg? When one tears, just pull on the spare third dangly leg. I'm not sure where it dangles, though.

Spider escape system

From Great Britain: a mini-ladder with suction pad to help spiders climb out of the bath.

Flatulence de-odorising pad

A small charcoal pad positioned inside the wearer's knick-knacks at the rear to soak up the pong from gassy trumps. Yes, it's a fart de-smeller!

Brassiere with integrated liquids pouch

Right, well, this is a bra that dispenses drinks, complete with straw.

Portable nasal mucus removing device

It has a handle, it has a probe and it has a motor. True, someone has developed an automatic nose picker. It works like a mini-vacuum to suck snot out of your nostrils, apparently.

It was never going to work

These seemed like a good idea at the time and most of them were actually made, but were they just way too wacky?

The Jumping Jeep
A 4x4 with twelve mini downward-facing propellers that would enable it to leap over obstacles such as fences, fallen trees and sunbathers. Hmmm...

Blue ketchup
A major food maker sold blue, purple, pink, orange and green ketchup for a short while. Interesting...

Spray-on hair
For men with an unwanted bald patch this black sooty stuff in a can was supposed to be the answer.

Flying tanks
Someone, somewhere in the military thought it would be a good move to put wings on tanks so they could fly to battles.

Smell-o-vision
A cinema system of the 1960s which released pongs during films. It stank.

Cat wigs
Wigs for cats. There's not much more to say.

Great inventor, silly invention

Some people gush forth brilliant ideas like a fountain. The inventors below all came up with hundreds of great designs and developments but, just occasionally, they also had an off day...

Leonardo da Vinci

An astonishingly talented artist, thinker and engineer, Leonardo came up with designs for the parachute, helicopter, tank and many other things over 400 years before they were made. But he also thought of inflated shoes to walk on water and they just don't work.

Thomas Edison

Edison invented an amazing number of useful things including the record player and movie camera but he also thought that concrete furniture was a good idea, even proposing that a concrete piano could be made. Fortunately, no one agreed with him – imagine cracking your knee on *that* armchair...

Clive Sinclair

This British genius of the electronic world made the first really small calculator as well as an affordable mini-computer and lots of other useful gizmos. Then, in the 1980s, he unveiled the Sinclair C5, a battery-powered plastic tricycle for adults. It was steered underneath the knees and looked like a broken vacuum cleaner.

Chindōgu: brilliant silliness from Japan

Japanese inventors love Chindōgu. This is the art of inventing things that are clever and sometimes silly all at the same time. You can find pictures of these on the Internet:

Baby mop – a romper suit with dangly bits so a baby cleans the floor as it crawls.

Napkin pants – trousers with towelling on the back to wipe your hands while eating.

Toilet roll hat – able to dispense continuous tissue for hay fever sufferers.

Booger keeper – nostril plugs for when your nose is just too leaky.

Portable zebra crossing – carry it rolled up through town and cross any road when you like.

Drymobile – a clothes line on top of the car to get those undies dry during long journeys.

Games that bombed?

People are inventing new games all of the time. Some people think the games on this page are good, but they also received lots of bad reviews...

Spawn of Fashan

This was a fantasy role-playing game of the 1980s. Reviewers at the time thought it was so bad that they were convinced it must be some kind of joke. It wasn't.

Doggie Doo Game

Yup, there really is a board game where you keep on squeezing the lead of a plastic dog until it plops on the table and you have to clear it up. Why?

Ninjabread Man

A 2007 video game. The box said, 'Candy Land is under attack by hordes of snapping cupcakes, angry bees, and jelly monsters that have taken over the land. Ninjabread Man must stop the evil army of monster cakes.' Right...

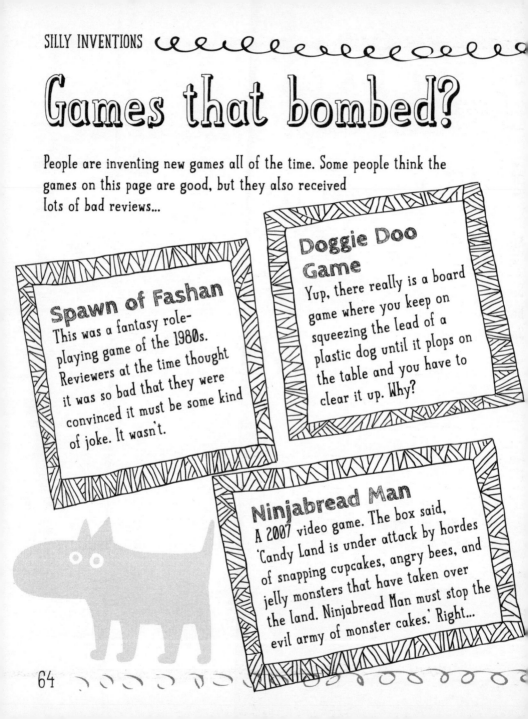

Technological innovations with a twist

Some manufacturers think that any invention can be improved by adding a motor, lights or sound. Sometimes they can, sometimes they can't...

Motorised ice cream cone: come on, it saves you from having to turn your ice cream when you lick!

Self-stirring mug: yes, it stirs your coffee for you – that is seriously lazy.

Laser-guided scissors: just in case you don't know where to cut.

Piano tie: well, who hasn't wanted a musical tie that plays tunes? Bargain.

Battery ear dryer: for when a towel just won't do.

Toast tattoos: hey, this is something we've all dreamed about, isn't it?

Illuminated slippers: never get lost when you go for a wee in the night.

Star Wars pizza cutter: it makes sounds like R2D2 while you slice, obviously.

Unusual gadgets

Brilliant or silly? You decide...

Condiment gun: shoots ketchup or mustard onto your BBQ sausage.

Half-spoon: it's a spoon cut in half longways – to cut down on calories, of course.

Backwards clock: well, it's a clock with the numbers the wrong way round.

Remote control tarantula: for giving your little sister the shock of a lifetime...

Water bomb catapult: now you can soak someone from around 91 metres away.

Dumb bell cutlery: for getting you fit as you consume a large pie.

Tattoo sleeves: roll-on nylon arm art to really freak out your granny.

Potty products

For some reason, it's very hard to find
these items in the shops:

* Lead balloon
* Tartan paint
* Inflatable dartboard
* Concrete trampoline
* Camouflaged golf ball
* Glass hammer
* Left-handed screwdriver
* Non-stick glue
* Bullet-proof soup
* Chocolate kettle
* Knitted light bulb

SILLY SPORTS

Commentator gaffes

Sports commentators and players do sometimes put their foot in their mouth and here are some suitably silly examples that have been reported over the years:

'Goalkeepers aren't born today until they're in their late twenties or thirties.'

Kevin Keegan (football)

'I owe a lot to my parents, especially my mother and father.'

Paul Hamm (gymnastics)

'There's nothing wrong with the car except that it's on fire.'

Murray Walker (F1)

'And the line-up for the final of the Women's 400-metre hurdles includes three Russians, two East Germans, a Pole, a Swede and a Frenchman.'

David Coleman (athletics)

'The doctors X-rayed my head and found nothing.'

Dizzy Dean (baseball)

'That's cricket, Harry, you get these sort of things in boxing.'

Frank Bruno (boxing)

Odd Olympic stories

Olympic athletes come in all types: the big, the strong, the fast and the silly...

Milo of Croton

Milo was a wrestler who, like all Olympic athletes of Ancient Greece, competed in the nude. Sadly, legend has it he got his hand stuck in a tree and was eaten by wolves.

Fred Lorz

American runner Fred was delighted to cross the finishing line first at the 1904 marathon. He was less pleased when people discovered that he'd been given a lift for 11 miles in his manager's car...

Dora Ratjen

Dora competed in the 1936 women's high jump competition, finishing a creditable fourth. So what? Well, the problem was that 'Dora' was really a bloke called Horst!

Barry Larkin

At the opening ceremony of the 1956 Olympics in Australia, everyone cheered when a runner entered the stadium with a torch. What they didn't know was that this was a prankster called Barry Larkin holding a wooden chair leg topped with a tin can and some burning knickers.

Eddie 'The Eagle' Edwards

Britain's only Olympic ski jumper, Eddie competed at the 1988 Winter Olympics. He was really too large for the event, had poor eyesight and couldn't afford the proper equipment. He finished last.

Curious sports

Are these really sports? We'll leave you to decide.

Bed racing

- Six push, one 'sleeps'.
- The course is 4km.
- The racers also have to cross a river with the bed.

Bog snorkelling

- Competitors are timed along a muddy trench wearing a snorkel and flippers.
- Swimming strokes are banned.

Toe wrestling

- Players try to trap their opponents' feet.
- The World Championships are held in a pub in Derbyshire.
- Alan 'Nasty' Nash is the current champion.

Hide-and-seek

- An official sport in Japan.

- For two teams of seven, usually played in woods, with complicated rules.

- It has been proposed as a future Olympic event.

Demolition derby

- A motorsport involving old bangers in a field.

- Cars smash into each other deliberately.

- The winner is the last car still moving.

Wife carrying

- Very popular in Finland.

- Big blokes race with their missus on their shoulder.

- The winners receive beer.

71

Sports fails: assorted blunders, mishaps and glitches

Sport has its moments of triumphs and glory and there are also the times that those involved would rather forget. You can find videos of most of these online.

Going up... going down

In 1999 Bradford City won promotion to the Premier League. The club captain Stuart McCall decided to address celebrating fans outside the ground by standing on the roof of a car. He fell off.

Countless wins

Motorcycle racer Riccardo Russo was well ahead of the pack when he crossed the finish line at the Italian Championship. He slowed down and punched the air in triumph. The trouble was, there was still one lap to go. The other riders zoomed past him.

That sinking feeling

John Bertrand's yacht, worth several million dollars, was racing in the Americas Cup in perfect conditions. Then, for no obvious reason, it snapped in half and sank in two minutes 15 seconds. You won't be surprised to learn that John didn't win the race.

My cup runneth over

Good: Real Madrid won the Spanish Cup in 2011 and paraded it through the city in an open-top bus. Bad: Sergio Ramos dropped the trophy and the bus ran it over.

Freak results

In most team sports the games are usually close but just occasionally one side gives the other an almighty trouncing resulting in a silly score. Or, even rarer, there's a close match with a barmy outcome. Here's a nice mix of both:

Sport	Year	Result
Football	1957	Charlton 7 Huddersfield 6
Basketball (NBA)	1983	Detroit Pistons 186 Denver Nuggets 184
Rugby League	1994	Barrow 138 Nottingham City 0
Cricket	1997	Sri Lanka 952 for 6 vs. India
Football	2001	Australia 31 American Samoa 0
Rugby Union	2002	Argentina 152 Paraguay 0
Ice Hockey	2008	Slovakia 82 Bulgaria 0
Football	2013	Plateau United Feeders 79 Akurba 0*

*This result was investigated by the Nigerian Football Federation after the home team (who needed to boost their goal difference to win promotion) suspiciously scored 72 goals in the second half. All the players were suspended.

Astonishing Olympics

The Olympic Games is supposed to be the greatest sporting event on the planet. And over its history, some astonishing things have happened...

Year	Venue	What happened?
1900	Paris	The winner of the marathon appeared to take a different course through the streets of the city to the other runners.
1904	St Louis	Only 12 countries turned up and only six women competed in the whole Olympics!
1912	Stockholm	One of the men's wrestling semi-finals matches lasted for over 11 hours. The winner was too tired to compete in the final.
1932	Los Angeles	The USA lost all of its hockey matches but still got a medal because only three teams entered the event.
1948	London	The UK was broke after World War II and sports kit was in short supply. However, a British store gave away free underpants to every male athlete.
1960	Rome	In the marathon all of the athletes wearing shoes were beaten by a runner in bare feet called Abebe Bikila of Ethiopia.
1996	Atlanta	Known as the Redneck Olympics, the opening ceremony featured 30 pickup trucks, and the only drink on sale was Coca Cola.

Manky mergers

A newspaper owner once suggested that it would be a good idea to combine two league football clubs, Reading and Oxford United, to make a new team called Thames Valley Royals. The idea was apparently laughed out of town by supporters of the clubs. Here are some more unlikely mergers and the new footy clubs that could result:

Arsenal + Barcelona = **Arselona (Or Barcenal)**

Partick Thistle + Sunderland = **Thistleland**

Crystal Palace + Millwall = **Palace Wall**

Burnley + Portsmouth = **Burnmouth**

Queen's Park Rangers + Motherwell = **Queen Mother**

Crystal Palace + Nottingham Forest = **Crystal Forest**

Heart of Midlothian (Hearts) + Accrington Stanley = **Heart of Stanley**

Real Madrid + West Ham = **Real Ham**

SILLY NAMES

Real names (but comedy ones)

OK, if your surname is Banger, that's unlucky, but DON'T call your baby son Ed. Yet, that is exactly what a mother and father from Somerset did in the 1600s. These are all real names taken from official lists such as birth registers:

Lorna Mower
Joe King
Stan Still
Ewan Mee
Ann Teak
Luke Warm
Mona Lott
Tim Burr
Robin Banks
Gail Force
Lou Paper
Ima Pain
Cliff Hanger

Names of big numbers

There are some really strange names for big numbers. Very large numbers have lots of zeros so they are written in a kind of shorthand like this:

Sextillion = 10^{21} = one followed by twenty-one zeros = 1,000,000,000,000,000,000,000

Here are some more real names for big numbers:

Nonillion (10^{30})

Undecillion (10^{36})

Quattuordecillion (10^{45})

Vigintillion (10^{63})

Googol (10^{100})

Googolplex (10^{Googol})

Wacky band names

Back in the 1940s pop groups had sensible names like The Andrews Sisters but the arrival of rock 'n' roll changed all that and things began to get a little bit silly in the 1960s with bands like The Kinks, Herman's Hermits and Grateful Dead. By the 1970s, nutty names for groups were quite normal and today there are hundreds of bands with outrageous names. Here are some good ones, old and new:

Bonzo Dog Doo Dah Band
Ned's Atomic Dustbin
Half Man Half Biscuit
Bowling for Soup
Angry Salad

Big White Undies
Crispy Ambulance
Hitler Stole My Potato
Planet of Pants
Zombies Under Stress

Footballers with funny names

This page contains a list of some funny footballer's names from around the planet (past and present). Some of these names are perfectly sensible in different countries, they just sound funny to English speakers.

*You won't believe it, but Wolfgang Wolf was once the coach of Wolfsburg FC.

Danny Diver	Scotland
Wolfgang Wolf*	Germany
Ruud Boffin	Belgium
Diaw Doudou	Senegal
Brian Flies	Denmark
Danger Fourpence	Zimbabwe
Roberto López Ufarte	Spain
Mark de Man	Belgium
Naughty Mokoena	South Africa
Harry Daft	England
Johnny Moustache	Seychelles
Mario Eggimann	Switzerland

Sporting nicknames

Sports fans from around the world like nothing better than a nutty nickname:

Sport	Nickname	Real name	Sports player info
Athletics	**The Flying Housewife**	Fanny Blankers-Koen	Dutch runner who won four gold medals at the 1948 Olympics. A biography of her was called *A Queen with Men's Legs*.
Basketball	**Dr Dunkenstein**	Darrell Griffith	Legendary US points scorer famed for his long-distance shooting.
Cricket	**The King of Spain**	Ashley Giles	English bowler – a set of mugs were made for him which should have said 'King of Spin' but came out wrong...
Cycling	**Hoycules**	Chris Hoy	Beefy Scottish sprint king, now Sir Chris, who is the most successful Olympic cyclist ever with six gold medals.
Darts	**The Power**	Phil Taylor	Reckoned to be the best darts player of all time, with 16 World Championship wins.

Sport	Nickname	Real name	Sports player info
Football	**The Ginger Ninja**	Paul Scholes	Red-haired Man Utd midfielder, famous for his passing ability and ludicrous number of bookings.
Rugby	**The Raging Potato**	Keith Wood	Irish hooker called 'The Potato' because of his bald noggin, and 'Raging' because of his brutal tackling. So now you know.
Skiing	**The Herminator**	Hermann Maier	Hefty Austrian downhill racer who had a scary crash at the 1998 Olympics, landing on his head at 70mph, before standing up and going on to win two golds.
Snooker	**Sheriff of Pottingham**	Anthony Hamilton	Well, he's good at potting snooker balls and he's from Nottingham, so...
Snowboarding	**The Flying Tomato**	Shaun White	Thought to be the world's best snowboarder (and maybe skateboarder too), this American dude got his nickname because of his huge red hair.
Tennis	**Boom-Boom**	Boris Becker	German who won Wimbledon aged just 17 – his big booming serve led to the nickname.

Real names (but simply preposterous)

Everyone has a name. There are lots of good names to choose from, and we laughed at a few silly ones on page 76. But why, oh, why did some parents see fit to call their kids *this*?

Daffy Dingle	Nutty Bullock
Frank Stank	Major Dork
Baldy Wiggins	Billy Silly
Charity Puke	Neptune Skidmore
Pinky Bottoms	Minnie Fart
Lotta Poo	Cosmo Crum

Shop Puns

These are all real shops or businesses.

All Cisterns Go - plumbers

Beauty and the Beach - tanning studio

William the Concreter - builder

Planet of the Grapes - wine store

The Codfather - fish and chips

Seymour Clearly - window cleaners

My Mother's Bloomers - flower shop

Buy One Get One Free - shoe shop

Fill Me Up Scotty - café

Wok Around the Clock - Chinese restaurant

Curl up and Dye - hairdressers

The land of the posh

'Toffs' often have cracking silly names and these are all real ones from the stately homes of Britain in the past:

Gilbert Elliot-Murray-Kynynmound, 1st Earl of Minto

With a tasty triple-barreller, Gilbert was a Scottish MP and friends with Edmund Burke (owner of another fine name) before gaining the impressive title of 'Envoy-Extraordinary to Austria'.

Sir Fitzroy Hamilton Anstruther-Gough-Calthorpe

An English Baronet who probably spent most of his life trying to cram his name onto cheques.

Clementina Elizabeth Drummond-Willoughby

This English aristocrat's name wasn't considered posh enough so was changed to Clementina Elizabeth Heathcote-Drummond-Willoughby in 1872.

Sir Reginald Aylmer Ranfurly Plunkett-Ernle-Erle-Drax

Owner of no less than a quadruple-barrelled name, Reg was an admiral in the Royal Navy who worked in Moscow in the 1930s with Ian Fleming, the author of the James Bond novels.

Royal monikers

Here are kings, queens, emperors and other assorted rulers who, for various reasons, were landed with some RIDICULOUS nicknames...

Charles the Bald
(Charles II of France)
Died 877. Yes, you guessed, he had a chrome dome.

Ivaylo the Cabbage
(Ivaylo of Bulgaria)
Died 1281. An emperor who started out as a pig herder, which probably involved cabbages...

Wilfred the Hairy
(Wilfred I of Urgell)
Died 897. A posh land-owning count who ruled part of Spain and who apparently looked like a walking ball of fluff.

Bloody Mary
(Mary I of England)
Died 1558. Queen who had lots of people put to death because she didn't like their church. Seems a tad unfair.

Farmer George
(George III of Britain)
Died 1820. A jolly king who liked nothing better than growin' a bit o' barley and keepin' a few sheep, arrr.

Louis the Fat
(Louis VI of France)
Died 1137. French monarch who actually started as thin but became a bit too fond of the palace pies, it seems (and the rest is history).

Old Copper Nose
(Henry VIII of England)
Died 1547. Remember this geezer? Six wives? He ordered copper to be added to silver coins. This showed through on the king's hooter, hence his ace nickname.

Silly Billy
(King William IV of UK)
Died 1837. This king liked sailing and making long, boring speeches which made no sense and earned him his fine nickname.

Ivan Moneybags
(Ivan I of Russia)
Died 1340. This Prince of Moscow made a packet taxing locals.

Ethelred the Unready
(Ethelred II of England)
Died 1016. Some people are just never ready, eh? But, sadly, his name really means 'bad counsel'. He became king when he was only ten. Ten!

Vlad the Impaler
(Vlad III of Wallachia)
Died 1476. The original Dracula, this Bulgarian ruler is remembered for skewering his enemies on sharp poles. Nice chap.

The Tennis King
(Gustav V of Sweden)
Died 1950. An old-school Swedish ruler who loved a game of tennis. He even represented his country at the sport, playing under the false name 'Mr G'.

Misheard names

Whoops! The public do sometimes get these famous people's names wrong...

Real name	Misheard as	Who is the real person?
Agatha Christie	**Agatha Crispie**	Famous writer, creator of *Poirot*.
Sir Bob Geldof	**Sir Bob Gandalf**	Singer and founder of Live Aid.
John Logie-Baird	**John Yogi-Bear**	Inventor of television.
Luther Vandross	**Loofah Vandross**	American soul singer.
Tracey Emin	**Tracey Eminem**	British artist.
Michael Portillo	**Michael Tortilla**	Former MP, now TV and radio presenter.
Kelsey Grammar	**Kelsey Grandma**	Actor who voices Sideshow Bob in *The Simpsons*.
Orson Welles	**Awesome Welles**	Major US film director and actor.
Bruce Forsyth	**Bruce Foresight**	Chintastic host of *Strictly Come Dancing*.
Dustin Hoffman	**Dustbin Hoffman**	Film actor, big in the 70s and 80s. Now normal size.

SILLY FILMS AND TV

Angry Beavers   Bumpety Boo
Captain Kangaroo   Dirty Jobs
Everybody Hates Chris
Fraggle Rock   Goof Troop
Hi Hi Puffy AmiYumi
I Pity the Fool
Just the Ten of us!
Kick Buttowski: Suburban Daredevil
My Family's got GUTS
National Bingo Night
Oggy and the Cockroaches
Quick Before They Catch Us
Splatalot!
Turkey Television   Unfabulous
Voltron: Defender of the Universe
Who Wants to Be a Superhero?
Xuxa   Yo Gabba Gabba!
Zoboomafoo

A list of real but strange sounding telly programmes from around the world.

Weird sounding TV shows

When subtitles go bad

Subtitles help deaf people to enjoy TV. They are spoken words appearing as text on the screen, and usually they are accurate but when a live broadcast is made they can go a bit wrong:

Subtitles should have said

Subtitles actually said

The sale of millions of poppies in Britain for Remembrance Day

The sale of millions of puppies in Britain for Remembrance Day

There should be a few more mist and fog patches

There should be a few more mist and fox patches

Subtitles should have said

The Labour leader
Ed Milliband

John McCain is 72 years old

We'll now have a
moment's silence for
the Queen Mother

Arsenal defender Bacary Sagna
is fouled by Patrice Evra

Prince William and the
Duchess of Cambridge
attended a film premiere

Subtitles actually said

The Labour leader
Ed Miller Band

John McCain is 672 years old

We'll now have a
moment's violence
for the Queen Mother

Arsenal defender Bacary Sagna
is fouled by a zebra

Prince William and the
badgers of Cambridge
attended a film premiere

The world of Tom and Jerry

The original series of these stupendous short cartoon films (made from 1940–1957) won seven Oscars and became one of the most loved TV programmes ever. It does, however, portray a very peculiar world, as these examples show:

Tom and Jerry live in an ordinary house but the house contains surprising amounts of explosives, axes, poison, mallets, fireworks and anvils.

A cat and mouse can read and write, create ingenious contraptions, handle deadly weapons, dress up, smoke, play musical instruments and make furniture but they cannot talk.

They talk sometimes.

Jerry is astonishingly strong for a little mouse.

Jerry manages to do the following to Tom: slice him in pieces, blow him up, hammer him into the ground, seriously burn him, freeze him, squash him with massive weights and electrocute him. Yet Tom never dies and there's not even a single drop of blood.

Humans' bodies are shown but not heads.

Tom regularly destroys the house trying to capture Jerry yet his owners keep him as a pet.

The worst film titles ever

Or maybe these are the best? You decide.

- **Attack of the Killer Tomatoes**
- You Only Live Twice
- **The Sisterhood of the Travelling Pants**
- When Father Had the Gout
- **She's the Man**
- Old Lady 31
- **Ghost in the Invisible Bikini**
- Santa Claus Conquers the Martians
- **I'm an Explosive**

Live TV blunders and shockers

Most television programmes are recorded and then edited before being broadcast but occasionally telly goes out live which greatly increases the chances for things to go silly.

Blue Peter Lulu poo-poo 1969

Lulu the baby elephant was brought into the BBC studio by a keeper but she did not behave herself in front of the cameras, first weeing then pooing right next to Valerie Singleton before standing on John Noakes' foot. The YouTube video is a must.

Emu attacks Parky 1976

Michael Parkinson was a respected TV interviewer who made the mistake of inviting guest Rod Hull to bring his puppet Emu to the chat show. Emu bit Parky on the leg, knocking him off his chair then pulling off his shoe. He survived, just.

Fishy hurricane 1987

Weatherman Michael Fish said that a woman had called the BBC because she'd heard that a hurricane was on the way to Britain. 'Don't worry, no there isn't,' said Mr Fish, going by the information he had. That night, a hurricane arrived with winds of 120mph in England. It blew down around 15 million trees, broke power lines, damaged buildings and caused shipwrecks. Oops.

Wrong man on the news 2006

Guy Goma turned up at the BBC TV Centre in London for a job interview. By mistake, he was hurried into a studio, put in a chair with a microphone, and questioned live on a news programme by a presenter who thought he was an expert in technology. Poor Guy did his best to answer the questions, thinking that it was a very odd job interview.

What Hollywood has taught us

You might believe that the following silly things that happen in films are true:

Cars that crash always burst into flames.

A single match will light up a huge cave or tunnel.

Villains prefer very complicated and expensive ways to kill people.

You can park right outside any building, however important.

Giant monsters can sneak up on people.

Baddies with machine guns are always a terrible shot.

Life is full of fast-talking, wisecracking characters who look odd but have a heart of gold.

A group of attackers will always wait patiently in turn to fight.

Criminal masterminds can always get planning permission to hollow out a volcano.

Top 7 Basingstoke films

Lawrence of Basingstoke

Four Weddings and a Basingstoke

Indiana Jones and the Temple of Basingstoke

Once Upon a Time in Basingstoke

Basingstoke 2

Finding Basingstoke

A Fish Called Basingstoke

★ ★ ★ ★ ★ ★ ★ ★ ★

SILLY WORDS

Splendid obsolete or archaic words

These words are either no longer used (obsolete) or
they are old words now rarely used (archaic) but, in any
case, they have a satisfying hint of silliness.

WORD	MEANING	WORD	MEANING
Pelf	Riches	Ostler	Stable worker
Skybosh	Tomfoolery		
Fuzzle	To make drunk	Snirtle	Laugh with snorts
Sloom	Sleep gently	Quagswag	Shake to and fro
Monsterful	Extraordinary		
Twattle	Gossip	Sooth	Truth
Lant	Stale urine	Mayhap	Perhaps

Ludicrously long words

Try saying these...

Antidisestablishmentarianism

The longest word in major dictionaries (not counting technical, scientific or made-up words). It has 28 letters and a whopping 12 syllables and means a political movement that opposes the separation of the state church and the nation. So now you know.

Floccinaucinihilipilification

This is 29 letters long but is a coined word (made up). It means the habit of regarding something as being useless. You can hear how to say it on Wikipedia.

Supercalifragilisticexpialidocious

A 34-letter word created by two songwriters for the musical *Mary Poppins*. According to the film it means 'something to say when you don't know what to say'. Right...

Pneumonoultramicroscopicsilicovolcanokoniosis

Has 45 letters and is a disease caused by breathing in fine particles of dust from volcanoes. It was created in 1935 by a famous puzzler but has appeared in an American dictionary.

However, there are longer words. In fact they are too long to write here:

183 letters

A made up word from an Ancient Greek play meaning a kind of rare stew.

1,909 letters

A chemical substance that appears in a dictionary of technical terms.

189,819 letters

The chemical name for the protein titin (although this isn't in any dictionary and is not regarded as a real word by the people who compile them). It takes 3.5 hours just to say this word!

Words without rhymes

Many long words have no true rhymes but here are some short ones. I bet you still try and find a rhyme for them:

Iron
Olive
Secret
Sixth
Wolf
Bulb

Angry
Monster
Elbow

More words without rhymes

These words are claimed to have no rhymes but do have *obscure* rhymes:

film	(rhymes with pilm, a Scottish word for dust)
month	(rhymes with hundred-and-oneth)
music	(rhymes with anchusic, a type of acid)
orange	(rhymes with Blorenge, a Welsh hill)
purple	(rhymes with curple, a donkey's bottom)
silver	(rhymes with chilver, a female lamb)
toilet	(rhymes with oillet, an eyelet [a small, round hole])

Eton College glossary

Eton is an uber-posh boys' school, once attended by British Prime Minister David Cameron. It is nearly 600 years old and has its own words, developed by pupils:

Abracadabra	The school's academic calendar	Mesopotamia	A large sports field
Beak	A master (teacher)	Oppidan	A boy who is not housed in College
Burning Bush	An ancient lamp-post used as a meeting place	Pop	The school prefects
Div	A lesson	Slack Bons	Boys who don't play cricket or row
Dry Bobs	Cricketers	Specialists	Sixth-formers

What are you talking about?

Some English words are unknown in other countries. Here's a selection of British phrases that sound silly to others:

Argy-bargy	Fortnight	Loo	Throw a wobbler
Bob's your uncle	Grotty	Manky	Yob
Bonce	How do	Nosh	Zebra crossing
Chinwag	Jammy	Skint	
Estate agent	Knickers	Trainers	

I beg your pardon?

Americanisms are words and phrases used by the people of the USA that sometimes baffle or sound silly to others:

Math (maths)
Gotten (got)
Bangs (fringe)
Zip code (postcode)
Burglarize (burgle)
Period (full stop)

Zee (last letter of the alphabet)
Bathroom (toilet)
Pants (trousers)
Fries (chips)
Chips (crisps)

Language oddments, curiosities and no-nos

Here's a selection of things that we sometimes say or write which might just be silly:

Hyperbole

Exaggeration for effect:

'I've told you a million times'

'This bag weighs a ton'

'I could eat a horse'

'I'll die if I don't sit down soon'

'It's boiling outside'

Euphemisms

A way of saying something sensitive, rude or unpleasant:

Pop your clogs (die)

A bun in the oven (pregnant)

Being economical with the truth (lying)

Fell off the back of a lorry (stolen)

Spend a penny (go to the loo)

Lose your lunch (vomit)

Botty burp (fart)

Oxymorons

Two words that don't make sense together:

Half dead
Old news
Almost perfect
Sweet sorrow
Open secret
Dry lake

Tautologies

Saying the same thing twice, for example:

Free gift (all gifts are free, aren't they?)
Join together ('join' is enough)
PIN number (the 'N' stands for number)
Honest truth (it's either true or not)
Completely essential ('essential' will do)

Just wrong!

Avoid these at all cost:

Alot (it's two words)
Could of (you mean 'could have')
Most amount ('most' will do)
Anythink (eh?)

Corporate jargon

Bosses and managers at large companies sometimes like to use their own newly made words and silly phrases to show how clever and creative they are. This has many names: corporate jargon, buzzwords, business-speak, management lingo and commercialese. Here are a few examples:

Touch base – to meet with colleagues to discuss progress.

Doability – how realistic a proposal might be.

Blue sky thinking – imaginative ideas.

Alpha Geek – the Head of the IT department at a company.

Hypertasking – doing too many things at once.

Peel the onion – get to the heart of the matter.

Voluntold – to be asked to volunteer by a senior person (almost an order).

Open the kimono – to share information with an outside group.

Shoot the puppy – to make an unpopular decision.

Boil the ocean – attempting something too large.

A selection of Jamaican slang

Every country has its own informal way of speaking and the island of Jamaica in particular has lots of great slang words:

SLANG TERM	MEANING
Bang belly	Large stomach
Chakka-chakka	Messy
Do road	To go on a trip
Duppy	Ghost
Frowsy	Smelly
Iron bird	Aircraft
Maggle	Model
Mash up	Break
Mooma	Mother
Nuff	A lot
Patoo	Owl
Peenie wallie	Firefly

Know your abbreviations

Abbreviation	Wrong	Wrong	Right
BBC	Big Belly Channel	Best Before Christmas	British Broadcasting Corporation
DVD	Don't Vandalise Durham	Darth Vader's Dead	Digital Versatile Disc
GCSE	Grannies Can't See Everything	Great Chin, Shocking Ears	General Certificate of Secondary Education
ISBN	Is Sheila Better Now?	I Squashed Beckham's Nose	International Standard Book Number
MBE	My Bottom's Educated	Madonna's Bacon Exploded	Member of the Order of the British Empire
NATO	Never Annoy Ten-foot Owls	Nougat-Assisted Take-Off	North Atlantic Treaty Organisation
RSPCA	Recently Someone Poked Colin's Ankle	Raw Sewage Provides Curious Amusement	Royal Society for the Prevention of Cruelty to Animals
YMCA	Your Mother Can't Accelerate	You Mustn't Cook Astronauts	Young Men's Christian Association

SILLY IDEAS*

Crazy fads

There have been thousands of these including food fads, dance crazes and trendy toys. Here is a selection:

The mashed potato

A 1962 dance craze which involved lots of foot waggling.

Pet rocks

In the 1970s you could buy a stone in a box and keep it as a pet. Really.

Waterbed

A bed with a mattress filled with water, popular in the 1970s.

Goldfish swallowing

A strange craze of the 1930s where US students swallowed live goldfish.

Kilroy was here

A wartime cartoon craze: a big-nosed man was drawn on a wall with these words.

Boombox

A portable stereo music cassette player from the 1980s, also called a ghetto blaster.

Space dust

A fizzy sweetie product containing carbon dioxide, making it tingle in the mouth.

*Or are they? You decide.

Fashion trends

People have worn some bizarre things throughout history – here are some of the sillier examples of clothes that were once trendy:

Lamb chop hat

A famous designer of the 1930s created a hat for ladies that looked like a lamb chop (the hat looked like a chop, not the ladies). True style for people who liked meat on their head.

Zoot suit

In the 1940s, some men thought it was cool to wear suits with massive shoulders, giant lapels, tiny waists, long jackets and vast baggy trousers that tapered at the ankle. For a while it was cool.

Poet shirt

An item for fashionable British men of the 1960s, this shirt was loose with baggy sleeves and big frills on the front. It was considered to give the wearer a wild, romantic poet or pirate look.

Catsuit

One-piece, skintight, spandex, bright-coloured suits with zips were regarded as just the thing for the disco by some women in the 1970s.

Hammer pants

A phenomenon of the late 1980s made popular by rapper MC Hammer. They were mega-baggy with tight ankles and a comically saggy crotch. Oh, and they were shiny.

Rubbish predictions

It's a dangerous thing to stand up and say, 'I think this will happen in the future...' But lots of people have done it. Here are some of the worst reported predictions ever:

Computers of the future will weigh about 1.5 tons.
(Popular Mechanics Magazine, 1949)

The world will end on Dec 21st 2012.
(Ancient Mayan leaders, around 500 AD)

There's no chance that the iPhone is going to get any significant market share.
(Microsoft boss, 2007)

We don't like the Beatles sound – guitar music is on the way out.
(Decca Records, 1962)

The car has reached the limit of its development.
(Scientific American, 1909)

No woman will become Prime Minister in my time.
(Margaret Thatcher, 1974)

American families haven't got time for television.
(New York Times, 1939)

Conspiracy theories

A conspiracy theory is a belief that a group of powerful people (usually the government or secret agencies) have carried out a huge, naughty plan and somehow covered it up. Like these:

That Elvis is still alive. Lots of people claim to have seen him.

That a crashed UFO was found at Roswell, New Mexico. Then quickly hidden by the military.

That William Shakespeare didn't write all those plays. But we're not sure who did write them...

That NASA faked the moon landings. They filmed them all in a studio, apparently.

That President John F. Kennedy was assassinated by the CIA or the mafia (or possibly Cubans). Rather than the single, deranged gunman who was caught.

That a mega-long-lasting light bulb has been invented. But big companies won't let people have it because they want us to keep on buying light bulbs.

That the planet is controlled by giant reptiles that look like people.

Regrettable military plans

A lot of time in the past was spent fighting, invading, raiding, sieging and planning battles. Sometimes the plans of military leaders worked out, and sometimes they didn't...

Fall of the Aztecs

In 1521 the capital city of the mighty Aztec Empire, Tenochtitlan, was approached by a few hundred Spanish Soldiers led by Hernan Cortes. The Aztecs had 300,000 warriors, yet a few months later the Spanish had control of the city (and soon all of Mexico) due to blunders by the Aztec leaders.

Spanish Armada

In 1588 Spain decided to invade England with a fleet of 130 warships. Several were set on fire before they even left port and the rest were chased by English ships around Britain. They then hit a storm which wrecked many of the boats on the coast of Ireland. Only about 67 vessels returned to Spain.

Napoleon takes on Russia

In 1812, the great undefeated French general Napoleon decided to invade Russia. Oh dear. He sent in about 600,000 soldiers but the crafty Russians just retreated and waited for winter – they knew how cold it was going to be. The French ran out of food, froze and became exhausted. Less than a quarter of the army survived.

Charge of the Light Brigade

In 1854, the Crimean War between Russia and Britain (plus other nations) was raging. Somehow, an order got mixed up, leading to a group of cavalrymen on horseback armed with swords charging straight at a battery of heavy Russian guns. It didn't go well.

Potty parenting advice

What's the best way to look after a baby? In the past there have been some really odd answers to this question. This list will give you an idea of some of the nuttier tips from centuries ago.

The Battle of Isandlwana

In 1879, the British Empire was in full swing with soldiers deployed all over the world to defend new territories. The fearsome Zulu tribe of South East Africa didn't like their land being grabbed so they wiped out a well-armed column of 1,800 British troops using just spears and cow skin shields. Ouch.

○ It's alright to let children drink gin (despite it being very strong alcohol).

○ Never hug and kiss babies.

○ Newborns should be smeared in lard.

○ Never feed a baby in the night – you will spoil it.

○ Bouncing a child on your knee will wreck his or her nerves.

○ Blowing smoke in the baby's ear cures earache.

Comical Internet crazes

In recent years people with nothing better to do have generated considerable amusement by taking photos and videos of silly things. Search online to see examples of these (but don't do them yourselves):

Lion Kinging: lifting pet cats and scruffy dogs high into the air like Simba.

Yarn bombing: where knitters wrap up public objects like phone boxes in lots of wool.

Goating: inserting goat bleats into edited music videos of popular singers.

Baby mugging: creating an optical illusion to make a baby appear to be sitting in a cup.

Cat bearding: placing a cat's head over your chin to give the impression of facial hair.

Wacky solutions to everyday problems

Here are some silly (or are they clever?) answers to some annoying problems around the world:

Problem	Caused by	Where	Answer
Very stinky blocked sewers (main drains)	A shortage of water to wash the poo along.	Bulawayo, Zimbabwe	Order every household to flush their loo at the same time each Saturday to blast the smelly blockages away.
Bus passengers getting jolted about	Drivers going too fast.	Changsha, China	Hang a big shallow bowl of water next to the driver so he/she gets soaked when not driving smoothly.
Hungry student with no time to get food	Having to complete late essay at computer.	Universities worldwide	Wear hoodie back to front with hood down; fill hood with popcorn; munch as you type.
Global warming	Loss of forests and overuse of energy.	Earth	Vertical farming: high-rise greenhouses in cities to produce food and allow trees to be planted in fields.

Iffy political parties

In most countries the government is elected by people voting for political parties. The following are real political parties.

The Two-tailed Dog Party – Hungary
House Party – Belgium
Beer Lovers Party - Russia
Official Monster Raving Loony Party - UK
Donald Duck Party - Sweden
Fancy Dress Party – UK
McGillicuddy Serious Party – New Zealand
Rhinoceros Party - Canada
Save Arthur Simpson Library - UK

Things not to get pierced:

Wrists
Eyes
Lungs
Rubber gloves
Bike
Cat
Chemistry teacher

SILLY JOKES

Loopy creature gags

Animals are great subjects for jokes, partly because they don't know we're laughing about them.

What do you do if you find a snake in the toilet? Wait till he's finished.

Where does a grizzly bear sit in the cinema? Anywhere he likes.

Why are elephants all wrinkly?
Well, have you ever tried to iron one?

Which side of a monkey
has the most hair?
The outside.

What has 50 legs but can't walk?
Half a centipede.

Why do cats lick their bottoms?
Well, no one else will do it for them.

Why do rabbits have
fur coats?
Because they'd look
stupid in anoraks.

Why does Tigger smell?
He's always playing with Pooh.

Transport puns

A pun is a 'funny' wordplay using a word or phrase that has a double meaning. Most puns (especially dads' puns) are AWFUL. But these are really good!

A man crashed his expensive car into a tree and found out how the Mercedes bends.

All the forms of motor racing had a competition to see which was the fastest and Formula won.

Crossing the Atlantic on a Jumbo Jet is not plane sailing.

Hearse racing is dead good.

I couldn't work out how to fasten my seatbelt. Then it clicked.

The Queen bought a new limo but she had nothing to chauffeur it.

Watch out for whales – they eat fish and ships.

I went on a long bike ride and got wheely tyred.

Our school boarded the train before anyone else and took the best seats: first class idea.

Doctor doctor jokes

There are some shocking medical problems here, but the treatment is even worse:

Doctor doctor, my daughter is eight feet tall.
Don't worry, she'll soon grow out of it.

Doctor Doctor, my eyesight is getting worse.
You're right – this is the Post Office.

Doctor doctor, will you give me something for my nose?
No need – I already have one.

Doctor doctor, I'm suffering from amnesia.
Just take two of these and you'll forget all about it.

Doctor doctor, I keep getting a pain in my eye when I drink tea.
Try taking the spoon out.

Doctor doctor, I can't stop stealing things.
Take this medicine, and if it doesn't work get me an iPad.

Doctor doctor, I think I'm a piece of luggage.
Yes, you're an interesting case.

Doctor doctor, my son has a slice of pizza up his nose.
Mmm, sounds like he's not eating properly.

Doctor doctor, I've just swallowed a mouth organ.
It's a good job you don't play the piano.

Doctor doctor, I've been stung by a wasp – shall I put some cream on it?
There's no point – it'll be miles away by now.

Knock knock jokes

Ah, the joy of answering the door
and finding the world's most annoying
person there...

Knock knock.
Who's there?
Atch.
Atch who?
Bless you.

Knock knock.
Who's there?
To.
To who?
'To *whom*'!

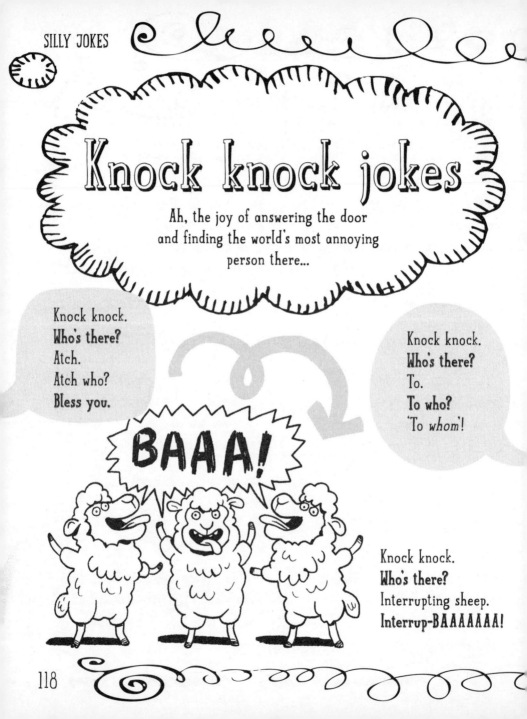

BAAAA!

Knock knock.
Who's there?
Interrupting sheep.
Interrup-BAAAAAAA!

118

Knock knock.
Who's there?
Uncle.
Uncle who?

Knock knock.
Who's there?
Uncle.
Uncle who?

Knock knock.
Who's there?
Uncle.
Uncle who?

Knock knock.
Who's there?
Aunt.
Aunt who?
Aunt you glad that Uncle's gone?

Knock knock.
Who's there?
Europe.
Europe who?
No, you're a poo.

Knock knock.
Who's there?
Cows go.
Cows go who?
No, cows go **Moo!**

Light bulb jokes

How many thieves does it take to change a light bulb?
What light bulb?

How many mystery writers does it take to change a light bulb?
Two: one to do most of the work then the other to give it a really good twist at the end.

How many jugglers does it take to change a light bulb?
One, but it takes at least three light bulbs.

How many tough guys does it take to change a light bulb?
None: tough guys aren't afraid of the dark.

How many drummers does it take to change a light bulb?
One... two, and a one, two, three, four.

How many weightlifters does it take to change a light bulb?
None: weightlifters only change heavy bulbs.

Chicken jokes

These are very old, but new ones keep appearing:

Why did the chicken cross the road?
It saw a zebra crossing.

Why did the chicken cross the playground?
To get to the other slide.

Why did the chewing gum cross the road?
It was stuck to the chicken's foot.

Why did the turkey cross the road?
It was the chicken's day off.

Why did the chicken cross the street?
The road was closed.

Why did the duck cross the road?
To prove it wasn't chicken.

Why did the rubber chicken cross the road?
To stretch its legs.

Mixed wit

Be warned: these jokes may make you laugh, howl, sob, run, scream, burp, dance or yodel.

Is that perfume I smell?
It is and you do.

What happened to that paper shop your mum opened?
It blew away.

This match won't light.
That's odd – it did this morning.

Can I try on that dress in the window, please?
Sorry, madam, you'll have to use the changing rooms.

What's the perfect cure for dandruff?
Baldness.

Do you have trouble making up your mind?
Well, yes and no.

What has a bottom at the top?
Your legs.

Come on, own up...

When someone trumps but no one owns up
then you must follow the golden rule (note,
'he' could be 'she'):

He who smelt it, dealt it.

He who denied it, supplied it.

He who detected it, projected it.

He who smelled it, expelled it.

He who knew it, blew it.

He who reported it, exported it.

He who spoke it, broke it.

He who exposed it, composed it.

He who unearthed it, birthed it.

He who sensed it, dispensed it.

He who rued it, brewed it.

He who quipped it, ripped it.

Annoying riddles

Riddles are cheeky little word puzzles with trick answers. See if your friends can work out any of these:

What goes up but never comes down?
Your age.

What part of a fish weighs the most?
The scales.

What is in December but no other month?
The letter d.

What gets wetter the more it dries?
A towel.

What can you put in a bucket to make it lighter?
A hole.

What belongs to you but others use it more than you?
Your name.

Mary's father has 5 daughters: Nana, Nene, Nini and Nono. What is the fifth daughter's name?
Mary.

What amazing invention enables you to see through walls?
A window.

Twelve one-liners

One liners are short, clever gags. Do you get these?

I wondered why the Frisbee was getting bigger,
and then it hit me.

Despite the cost of living, it remains popular.

Time is a great healer, but a terrible beautician.

I intend to live forever – so far so good.

Cannibals don't eat clowns because they taste funny.

I live in a £2m converted barn – unfortunately it was
converted into a bus shelter.

Hard work never killed anyone, but why take the risk?

Save the Earth: it's the only planet with chocolate.

Two wrongs don't make a right but three lefts do.

I started out with nothing and still have most of it.

Some people have a way with words, some not have way.

Seven fifths of all people struggle with fractions.

SILLY POEMS

Nutty wordplay

Get yourself a nice cup of hot chocolate, sit back,
put your feet up (no higher than the roof please)
and enjoy these little ditties that wangle and whiffle
words about like poetic ping pong.

Cheese and Crackers

Some people
Think
The Moon
Is made of
Cheese.

They must
Be
Crackers.

Andy Seed

I've Pegged A Fried Egg To The Table

I've pegged a fried egg to the table
and firmly affixed the French fries,
I've fastened the fruit and the fritters,
I've padlocked the peas and the pies.
I've jammed tight the jam tarts and jelly,
the chicken and cheesecake I've latched,
I've made sure to pin the pancetta,
the salad is safely attached.

The steak has a stake through its middle,
I've stapled the grapes and the greens,
I've made sure to skewer the strudel
and nail on the plate full of beans.
The tuna's now truly unyielding,
the cucumber can't be unscrewed...
whenever it comes to a mealtime,
I so love to bolt down my food.

Graham Denton

Bare bear

Why is a bear
Called a bear?
To see one clothed
Is very rare.

Andy Seed

Queue

I've stood in this queue
To go to the lueue
Since quarter past tueue
It's perfectly trueue
– Oh what shall I dueue?

Andy Seed

Algy Saw a Bear

Algy saw a bear;
The bear saw Algy.
The bear had a bulge;
The bulge was Algy.

Anon

The Rev Spooner's Shopping List

Jaspberry ram
Chot hocolate
Ninger guts
Beggie vurger
Sea poup
Spixed mice
Lairy fiquid
Bea tags
Pushroom mizza
Chini meddars
Jackcurrant belly
Poo laper
Nicken choodles
Haghetti spoops
Lire fighters
Glubber roves
Sup a coup
Poothtaste
Palf a hound of Chensleydale wheese
and
Baked beans
(Gank thoodness)

Andy Seed

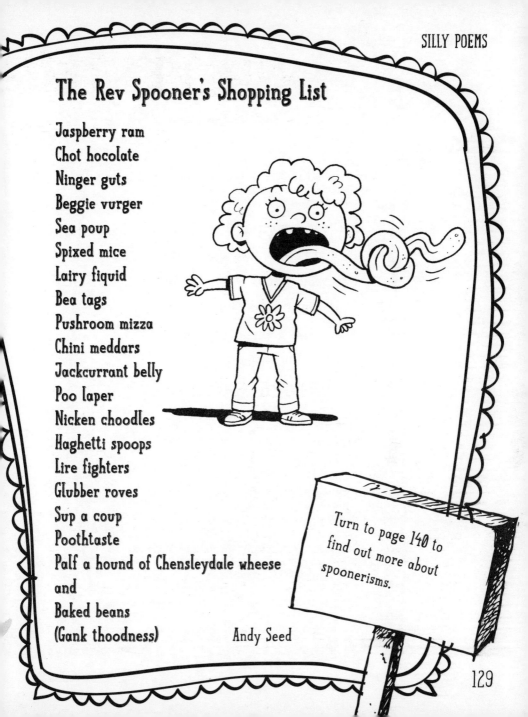

Turn to page 140 to find out more about spoonerisms.

Toast Story

Mike Barfield

I daren't go down to the kitchen
So I'm hiding up here in bed.
Last night, driven mad by hunger
I murdered a slice of bread.
I tore it away from its family -
That poor brown, innocent slice -
I rammed it down in the toaster
And burnt it alive in a trice.
Then when it popped up, expired,
I manhandled it out of its slot
Covered its corpse in butter
And devoured it piping hot.
Now, on cold dark nights in the winter
As I reach for the butter knife
I think of that slab of dead brown bread
That once was a slice of life.
So that's why I'm under these covers
I'm scared it's come back as a ghost
And my house will forever be haunted
By a phantom slice of toast.

Mighty Oak

Don't worry if your job is small
and your rewards are few;
Remember that the mighty oak
was once a nut like you.

Anon

Sporty Family

Dad's always wrestling (with the crossword);
Granny's brilliant at running (the bath);
Mum's good at curling (her hair);
Grandad loves bowls (of ice cream);
My brother's great at diving (into bed);
My sisters are experts at rowing (with each other);
And I'm very keen on polo (mints).
What a sporty family! (not).

Andy Seed

A noggle of nonsense

OK, noggle isn't really a word but it should be. Anyway, here are some silly nonsensical poems to enjoy.

If all the world were paper,
And all the sea were ink,
And all the trees were bread and cheese,
What should we have to drink?

Anon

Big Foot

Big foot,
Massive toes,
Huge eyes,
Tiny nose;

Long ear,
Giant tum,
Wide legs,
Smelly bum.

Andy Seed

In the Jelly Jungle

In the jelly jungle
Wild beasts and snakes
Make their dens in ice-cream caves
And sleep on chocolate cakes.

In the jelly jungle
The sausage-roll bird sings
Lays its eggs in spaghetti nests
And preens its syrup wings.

In the jelly jungle
The crocodile will doze
In a swamp of custard
With a cherry on his nose.

Jan Dean

Loopy limericks

Limericks are traditional five-line rhyming poems which have been popular for over two hundred years. Some are very rude but these are just silly.

Consider the poor hippopotamus:
His life is unduly monotonous.
He lives half asleep
At the edge of the deep,
And his face is as big as his bottom is.

Anon

There was a young lady of Ryde
Who ate some green apples and died.
The apples fermented
Inside the lamented
And made cider inside her inside.

Anon

Monet had style that was fearless,
Cezanne's use of colour was peerless,
But Gaugin was potty,
Seurat was spotty,
And Van Gogh? Well, he was just earless.

Andy Seed

There was a young man of Japan
Whose limericks never would scan.
When asked why this was,
He replied, 'It's because
I always try to fit as many syllables into the last line as ever I possibly can.'

Anon

Doggerel!

Doggerel is really dodgy poetry
and the undisputed master of it was
William Topaz McGonagall (1825–1902) who is widely
reckoned to have been the worst poet ever. He's so
bad that he's good. His poems were usually painfully
long, so here are some short extracts from a few.

From 'Grace Darling'

Oh! my kind father, you will surely try and save
These poor souls from a cold and watery grave;
Oh! I cannot sit to see them perish before mine eyes,
And, for the love of heaven, do not my pleading
despise!

Then old Darling yielded, and launched the little boat,
And high on the big waves the boat did float;
Then Grace and her father took each an oar in hand,
And to see Grace Darling rowing the picture was grand.

From 'Annie Marshall, the Foundling'

One day Matthew asked Annie if she would be his wife,
And Annie replied, I never thought of it in all my life;
Yes, my wife, Annie, replied Matthew, hold hard a bit,
Remember, Annie, I've watched you grow up, and
consider you most fit.

From 'Lines in Praise of the University of St. Andrews Liberal Association Annual Dinner'

And, as for the landlord, Mr Rusack, he's very kind,
Also Mrs Rusack; more kinder people would be hard to find,
I wish them every success for their kindness to me,
Long may they live, and their family.

SILLY THINGS TO DO

Silly things to say

When you feel an irresistible urge to be silly then consider some of the ideas below. You will drive yourself and others round the bend but, hey, that's part of the fun.

Tongue twisters

Have a go at these then try making up some of your own:

Three free throws

Sally Smith's Fish Sauce Shop

The boot black bought the black boot back

Ed had edited it

The Leith Police dismisseth us

Rubber baby buggy bumpers

Bad money mad bunny

Unique New York

Chop shops stock chops

One smart fellow, he felt smart;
Two smart fellows, they felt smart;
Three smart fellows, they all felt smart.

Nonsense languages

Vowel switch:

Replace one vowel with another to turn words into amusing gobbledygook. For example, if the only vowel was 'o', you could have **shroddod whoot** for breakfast, **fosh and chops** and **moshy poos** for lunch and watch **Ogghoods** or **Bog Brothor** on TV.

Unwinese:

Mangle some English for fun like old-school comedian Stanley Unwin. Here's how his version of *Goldilocks and the Three Bears* goes:
Goldyloppers trittly-how in the early mordy, and she falolloped down the steps.

Jabberwocky:

Lewis Carroll made up a whole load of words for his famous poem 'Jabberwocky' and you can do the same — try sticking the end of one word on the beginning of another for starters.

Spoonerise

A spoonerism is when you swap the beginning letters/sounds of two words in a phrase, for example 'par cark' (car park). They are named after The Rev W.A. Spooner who was famous for muddling up his words (see the poem on page 129). Some people say them by accident but it's fun to make them up too:

Pot Noodle › Not Poodle
wedding dress › dredding wess
monkey puzzle › ponkey muzzle

You can also do it with names:
Benny Jones › Jenny Bones
Polly Wood › Wolly Pood

Warning: words/names beginning with vowels mostly don't work, and names can turn rude, as Penny Hooper knows only too well!

Go backwards

Try saying your name backwards or the names of your friends, family or the famous. Not easy, eh? But quite silly. You could also reverse places or animals or supermarket products – or anything!

Silly games to play

You don't need anything to play these talking games, just a sense of humour and a friend or two.

Useless!
Have a look at the Potty Products on page 67 (glass hammer, lead balloon, etc.) and see if you can add some more to the list.

The Game of Tomorrow
Football is everywhere, so why not invent a better ball game: hairball, bellyball, chinball...

What's the worst?
What's the worst thing to...

Wear at a wedding?

Put in your sandwiches?

Take swimming?

Use to stir porridge?

Give to the queen?

Name a cat?

[Now make up some more.]

Merge-a-sport.
Devise some new sports by combining two old ones:

Pool + snooker = pooker (or snool)

Rugby + golf = gugby (or rolf)

Pun wars

Take turns with someone to out-pun them on a chosen subject:

Fish puns: Nice plaice you have here; speak up – I'm hard of herring; on yer pike!

Bird puns: Who's your gull friend? Rook at me when I'm talking; wren will you stop?

Car puns: You never Nissan, do you? Van shall we go home? Audi you do it?

Try animals, trees, clothes, foods, countries, towns or your own category.

Life on the road

A game for car journeys where you make up meanings for funny places on road signs:

Belper – a person who laughs far too loud.

Kettering – the crumbs left when you eat a pastry.

Troon – the sound a football crowd makes when a shot just misses the goal.

Reg expansion

Another agreeably silly game for a car journey where you create phrases using the first three letters on a passing car number plate:

CHM: camels hate Monopoly; come here mother; can't hoover measles.

EZJ: Elvis zaps jelly; eat zoo junk; everyone's zips jiggered.

TPY: totally pink yeti; trashed Paris yesterday; that pimple's yours.

Mean Meanings

Make up some words and then decide what they mean:

Yuffle
Mox
Vipperocity

Eggy story

I'm not sure why this is called eggy story but who cares, it's silly. You simply take turns to tell a story, speaking one word at a time. It has to make sense and it has to be funny. And if you can get the word 'eggy' in there, then all the better.

Update a proverb

One person says the first part of a well-known saying then everyone takes turns to add a new, silly ending (real answers after h, below):

a) Rome wasn't built in a .... (e.g. newsagent's; mood; curry)

b) The bigger they are .... (e.g. the harder they hit you; the more expensive their pants; the more portions for us)

Here are some to get you going:

c) Actions speak louder than ....

d) Don't count your chickens until ....

e) Two heads are ....

f) Beggars can't be ....

g) Where there's muck there's ....

h) You can't teach an old dog ....

[Real endings: a) day; b) the harder they fall; c) words; d) they are hatched; e) better than one; f) choosers; g) brass; h) new tricks].

Pencil and paper silliness

Some of these you can do on your
own but they are better shared.
You'll need a pencil and paper.

Potty person

Create a preposterous new person:

Draw him/her

Give your person a name

Add an address

**Write down his/her appearance, job,
friends, hobbies, hates, loves,
fave fashions, etc.**

Hopeless inventions

Sketch some funny but completely
useless gadgets:

Horse umbrella

Ruler trousers

Suitcase hat

Edible laptop

Loopy lists

Use these headings to make some laughable lists, then think of your own headings:

- Pointless hobbies
- Bad babysitters
- School report comments that teachers never make
- Alternative uses for sprouts
- Lies about cheese
- Arsenal should sign
- Inadvisable DIY projects
- Rubbish names for the next Vauxhall
- If you run out of shampoo, don't use...

Here's an example:

Mistakes to avoid when brushing your teeth

Using a lavatory brush

Putting toothpaste on the handle

Running the bath tap

Gargling before you start

Spitting on your foot

Brushing for more than six hours

Rinsing with custard

Design a daft day

Write down your timetable for the nuttiest day you can imagine. Here are some pointers:

Revolting breakfast
(e.g. Shredded Feet)

Pointless morning activity
(e.g. Pretend to be a gibbon for half an hour)

Gross lunch (e.g. Barfburgers)

A trip to a foolish fictional place
(e.g. Earwax World)

Watching a shocking TV programme
(e.g. Doctor Whaaaat!)

Text your friend your news
(e.g. Cleared out my bottom drawer – there were 3 bottoms in it)

Bed time read
(e.g. Diary of a Wimpy Squid)

Senseless signs

Make some silly signs and blu-tack them around the house, for example:

NO PARKIN
(on food cupboard)

CAUTION: THIS SIGN HAS SHARP EDGES
(to go anywhere)

DO NOT READ THIS SIGN (to go anywhere)

NO ENTRY
(put in the middle of a wall)

147

More silly things to do

A random selection of foolish fun:

Start a silly collection

If you were sensible you might collect stickers or stamps or fossils. If you were not sensible you might collect belly button fluff, photos of your big toe in odd places, or pieces of breakfast cereal that look like singers.

Attempt an 'impossible' challenge

Some of these are actually possible:

- Lick your elbow
- Raise just one eyebrow
- Twitch your nose
- Wiggle your ears
- Tickle yourself
- Move your eyes in opposite directions
- Circle your foot clockwise while circling your finger anti-clockwise

Play a classic prank

Just be careful about who you prank. Choose someone who is: a) smaller than you; b) in a good mood; c) not wielding a heavy club. But really, don't play a prank on anyone who will get upset.

Apple pie bed

Fold the bottom sheet of a bed back on itself so it's impossible to get in.

Rude welcome

Place a lightly inflated whoopee cushion under a door mat.

Foot squish

Put a piece of bread in the toe of someone's shoe.

Long letter

Fold a very long piece of paper along its length so that the end fits in an envelope. Half post the envelope through the front door, leaving the long piece of paper outside the door. Add a witty message to the long letter.

Naughty mouse

Change a person's computer mouse from right- to left-handed (or vice-versa).

Old news

Swap the inner section of today's newspaper with yesterdays' inner section.

MISCELLANEOUS SILLINESS

Witty tribute bands

Tribute bands are fake famous rock and pop groups who dress up and sound like the real thing. Here are some of the best named ones:

Bjorn Again (Abba)
Fred Zeppelin (Led Zeppelin)
By Jovi (Bon Jovi)
The Rolling Clones (The Rolling Stones)
No Way Sis (Oasis)
The Bootleg Beatles (The Beatles)
Elton Jack (Elton John)
New2 (U2)

Antarctic Monkeys (Arctic Monkeys)
Not the Hoople (Mott the Hoople)
Surely Bassey (Shirley Bassey)

Big mama boats and ships

The weight of boats and ships is normally given in tonnes, but that's far too sensible. Here are some much sillier ways to say how heavy they are:

Vessel	Weighs the same as
The Mayflower	3,000,000 eggs
The Golden Hinde	119 Honda Civics
Cutty Sark	6,600 donkeys
Titanic	650,000 Cliff Richards
The Bismarck	4 Eiffel Towers
Queen Mary II	375 million cans of pea and ham soup
Jahre Viking oil tanker	2.2 billion pairs of long johns

Ten common misconceptions

A misconception is a mistaken belief (a 'wrong fact'). Lots of people think that these silly things are true when they aren't.

That Christopher Columbus thought the Earth was flat. [Sailors in his time knew the planet was round.]

That Vikings wore horns on their helmets. [No evidence has ever been found for this.]

That the modern toilet was invented by Thomas Crapper. [He was a plumber who made some improvements to the flushing system.]

That the Great Wall of China can be seen from space. [No man-made object on the Earth has ever been seen by an astronaut.]

That bulls charge when they see the colour red. [Bright colours do not stand out to bulls.]

That bats are blind. [All bats have eyes and can see to some extent.]

That ostriches bury their head in the sand to hide from enemies. [They don't.]

That blood in human veins is blue. [It's always red.]

That swallowed chewing gum will clog up your guts. [It passes through the body just like food.]

That Frankenstein was a monster. [In the book, Victor Frankenstein was the monster's creator.]

Things novice scouts get sent to collect at camp

One of the oldest tricks in the book is to send someone new on a fool's errand. Poor lads who've never been away from home before are told to go and fetch one of these:

A long weight

A bubble for a spirit level

A second aid kit

A can of steam

Sparks for the camp fire

Dehydrated water

A bacon stretcher

The Stella Awards

The Stella Awards are presented to people who make outrageous legal claims. They are named after a woman who spilt a cup of coffee in her lap and took McDonald's to court. She was awarded nearly three million dollars.

2002

A passenger sued Delta Airlines for making him sit next to a very large man on a plane.

2003

A man who was hit by lightning made a claim against the theme park where it happened, saying that they should have warned him not to be outside during a storm.

2005

A practical joker smeared glue on a toilet seat in a DIY store. The man who sat on it demanded $3m compensation from the shop.

2006

A woman who was 'attacked' by a squirrel outside a shopping mall claimed a huge sum of money because the mall didn't warn her that there were squirrels living nearby.

Wheeled insanity

Mechanic who has nothing better to do +
slow vehicle + big engine = this:

Vehicle	Normal top speed	Fastest recorded speed
Quad bike	60mph	196mph
Tractor	20mph	75mph
Lawn mower	8mph	133mph
Mobility scooter	7mph	120mph
Shopping trolley	2mph	44mph
Sofa	0mph	101mph

Spend, spend, spend...

It's my money and I'll spend it how I like.

Lunacy

In 1980 an American called Dennis Hope wrote to the United Nations claiming that the moon belonged to him. Dennis never heard back so he began to sell one-acre plots of the moon for $36.50, giving buyers a certificate. So far he has sold 611 million acres to silly people (including to three former US presidents) even though it's obvious that he doesn't really own the moon.

Cheesy money

Diana Duyser thought that her cheese toastie looked like the Virgin Mary and so she kept it in a box for ten years. After it appeared on TV and the Internet, Diana put her famous snack on eBay and sold it for $28,000. Possibly the silliest sandwich in history.

Woodgate whoops

Footballer Jonathan Woodgate was bought by Real Madrid for over £13 million in 2004. Unfortunately he was injured and didn't play for a year. When Woodgate finally played his first game for Madrid in 2005 he scored an own goal and was sent off. Soon after, he was injured again and played only nine matches for the club in three years before being sold at a big loss.

> > > > > > > > > > >

Silly hairstyles

Hairstyles come and go.
Should these have come?

The bouffant – classic big hair (made walking difficult): favoured by US women in 1963.

Moptop – shaggy bowl-cut look from 1964: particularly bad around the ears.

Combover – the bald man's 'last strand', with pasted down side locks.

Mohican – punk cut of late 70s and beyond.

Footballer's perm – curly, bouncy and daft: as sported in the 1980s.

White dreadlocks – a dead octopus draped on your head: 3–4 people in 1992 thought it was good.

Outlandish book titles

Amazingly, these are all real books...

How to be Danish

COOKING WITH POO

Where Underpants Come From

BOMBPROOF YOUR HORSE

How to Live with an Idiot

Treat Your Own Neck

BE BOLD WITH BANANAS

DOES GOD EVER SPEAK THROUGH CATS?

ALL ABOUT SCABS

Whose Bottom is This?

Alternatives to a sleepover

Ideas for a silly night with friends:*

Cheepover	Spend the night with a load of budgies.
Creepover	Watch scary films until 2 a.m.
Leapover	Everyone jumps on your bed until it breaks.
Sheepover	All-night lamb dinner.
Sweepover	Bring a brush or mop.
Weepover	Communal girly sob about the break up of a cheesy boy band.

* Don't actually try these.

FURTHER INFORMATION

Books to read

If you like silly facts and amazing information then try some of these books:

Why is Snot Green? by Glenn Murphy (Macmillan, 2007)
Poo at the Zoo by Sarah Eason (Bloomsbury, 2012)
Big Pants, Burpy and Bumface by Russell Ash (Red Fox, 2013)
Fitter, Faster, Funnier Football! by Michael Cox (A & C Black, 2014)

Websites

More fun things to do online:

www.factmonster.com – just loads of information
www.funology.com/ – lots of things to do plus facts and jokes
http://www.nhm.ac.uk/kids-only/ – all sorts from the Natural History Museum
www.beano.co.uk – all sorts about one of the best comics ever
www.bbc.co.uk/newsround/ – scroll down for the latest strange news stories

AVAILABLE AUGUST 2014!

Warning: this book will cure all boredom!

Pick which pet is worse: a dead earwig, a flu germ or a T. rex? Decide what you would do if you were ruler of the world... plus many more amazing boredom-busting ideas!

This witty and wacky book is bursting with brilliantly funny games, jokes, quizzes, riddles and awesome things to do for hours of fun.

£5.99

978-1-4088-5076-3

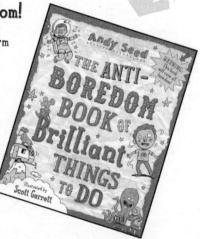